Also by Ellis Blackwood

"Among the finest historical cozy mysteries of our time" – *Cozy Crime Reads*

The Samuel Pepys Mysteries
Mr Pepys's Stolen Diaries (ellisblackwood.com)
Book 1: The Brampton Witch Murders
Book 2: The Plague Doctor Murders
Book 3: The Coffee House Murders
Book 4: The King's Court Murders
Book 5: The Frost Fair Murders
Book 6: The Drury Lane Murders
Book 7: The Brampton Ghost Murders
Book 8: The Crown Jewels Murders
Book 9: Jacob's Last Standish

The Quill & Page Victorian Mysteries

Book I: The Belgravia Phantom (summer 2026)
Book II: The Whitechapel Orphan (summer 2026)

The Frost Fair Murders

The Samuel Pepys Mysteries Book 5

Ellis Blackwood

Vintage Mystery Press

ISBN: 978-1-0687027-4-7

Cover design, editorial & historical fact-checking: Tim Brown, A.S.C. (Rtd).

Snowflake cover images by rawpixel.com.

For Tim & Debs, so very smug on their desert island.

Scan for website and social media links

Contents

Chapter One

Christmastide

It was Christmas Day, 1666, and as Samuel Pepys rose to carve the steaming rib of beef at the centre of the great oak dining table, a mouse darted across his foot.

"Gadzooks!" he exclaimed. "Foul vermin!"

Then hurriedly, noting the raised brows and pursed lips of his more pious guests, he apologised. "Beef, Mr Evelyn?" he asked, eyeing Abigail Harcourt, who was struggling to stifle a chuckle.

There were six around the table that day.

At the head sat Pepys, the host; to his right, Abigail, and beside her, Jacob Standish. Abby and Jacob were Pepys's personal inquisitors, tasked with investigating crimes and misdemeanours on his behalf. Jacob was a gangly sort, too tall for his own good, while she was small and neat. They made a successful, if unlikely, team.

What had begun as an informal arrangement had become a source of pride to Pepys, who relished the distinction it lent him.

Opposite Pepys, and to Jacob's right, was John Evelyn. Pepys and Evelyn were both members of the Royal Society - Evelyn, notably, a founding Fellow. They had first crossed paths the previous year while serving as Commissioners for the Sick and Wounded Seamen.

On being invited to dinner, Evelyn - much to Pepys's thinly veiled chagrin - had asked to bring two companions: Arthur Baines and Barnaby Barker. Baines, a recent acquaintance from his neighbourhood in Deptford, had expressed such eagerness to meet the estimable Clerk of the Acts to the Navy Board that Evelyn felt it only courteous to include him. Barker was Evelyn's grandfather.

These guests now occupied the remaining seats, opposite the inquisitors.

Baines was a haughty fellow with a sallow complexion, plain taste in fashion, and an old leather satchel that bore its maker's mark, 'H.W.'. Barker's skin was so lined, it was hard to discern his thin mouth; according to Evelyn, he was 88 years old, remembered the celebration bells of the Spanish Armada, saw Hamlet at the Globe and the funeral of Elizabeth I, and was profoundly deaf.

The church bell of St Olave's across the road chimed once as the kitchen maid, Mary Blythe, entered carrying a jug of wine. Her gaze lingered over the culinary delights spread across the table, then settled on her former colleague.

Abby quickly dropped her head, her flame-red ringlets falling forward to hide her reddening cheeks. Though her rise from servitude felt like a blessing from the Lord, it came with a gnawing unworthiness she could not entirely shake.

"Where is your wife, Sam?" Evelyn asked, helping himself to a slice of mince pie. "I was hoping to make her acquaintance."

More than a decade Pepys's senior, the eager-eyed, somewhat gaunt gentleman bore an expression of earnest conviction. Like his host, he was a man of learning - a keen gardener and authority on trees, as well as a staunch Anglican.

Pepys began choking on a mouthful of wine, prompting Baines to abandon his beef and deliver a hefty slap to his back.

"Much obliged to you," Pepys wheezed as Baines resumed his seat. "Aye, John, I too would have welcomed Elizabeth's company, but alas, the poor lady took a tumble on the ice this morning and is presently confined to her bed."

Abby set down her spoon. "I'm sorry to hear it, Mr Pepys. Is she injured? Should I attend to her?"

Pepys growled softly. "I have told you before, Abigail, you now serve as my inquisitor, not my servant. My wife's ankle is swollen, and her cheek is bruised; she did not wish to be seen thus in such esteemed company. She…"

Evelyn interjected, leaning forward. "Tell me, sir, what is the purpose of these… inquisitors? I confess, I have ne'er encountered such a profession."

Adjusting his shirt cuff with a half-smile, Pepys launched into an explanation. How Jacob's father, on his deathbed, had entrusted his son's future to Pepys, leading to Jacob's current service. And how Abigail, whom he had taken under his wing as his maid, had proven so adept at detection that he had promoted her to work alongside Jacob.

Taking a hearty swig of wine, Pepys continued, "Why, only recently, Jacob and Abigail were engaged in a case of murder at the King's court."

Jacob cast a wary glance at Abby. The dour-faced young man, whose unruly brown eyebrows met in the middle, knew all too well that King Charles had expressly forbidden them to speak of the events at Whitehall Palace.

Beside him, he noticed Abby's jaw tighten.

They had passed on the King's warning to Pepys, however, given his natural ebullience - and the tongue-loosening properties of the alcohol - he appeared entirely to have forgotten.

"Would you believe, John, that I, Clerk of the Acts to the King's Navy, was implicated in the murder," Pepys went on, gesturing with a half-eaten beef rib, "of one of His Majesty's...?"

The shattering of Abby's Delftware plate on the floor silenced him abruptly, as all assembled stared at her aghast. Apologising - though that was, in truth, no accident - Abby knelt to retrieve the shards just as Mary Blythe's hurried footsteps echoed up the staircase.

With attention diverted, the inquisitor seized the chance to whisper furtively in Pepys's ear. His hand flew to his mouth in horror, and with the other, he pushed his goblet aside.

After a brief delay, the meal resumed, and Baines spoke up. "The Navy Board, you say, Mr Pepys? A most vital office in these troubled times, and one that surely demands a keen mind."

Pepys nodded, polishing his fingernails on his doublet, as Baines continued, "And with the Dutch so emboldened of late. No doubt they fear our great nation's might at sea. Yet I wonder... does His Majesty seek peace in the Dutch War?"

Retrieving his goblet, Pepys swirled his wine. "The King is ever prudent, Mr Baines. He knows that strength commands respect."

Baines grinned, eyes alight. "Then we shall break their fleet upon the waves, blast their galleons to splinters, and send their men to the deep! Nay to peace, sir, and nay to surrender!"

Pepys shot to his feet, goblet raised. "A toast to His Majesty and to our glorious England!"

Only Mr Barker failed to rise, stooped so low over the table that his chin was almost in his gravy, intent on spearing a troublesome turnip. When his grandson nudged him, he glanced up, saw everyone else standing and creakily followed suit.

When they sat, Abby turned Barker. "I'm eager, sir, to hear your tales of Good Queen Bess…"

But the ancient gentleman had returned to his turnip.

"I fear he cannot hear you, Abigail," Evelyn cut in, casting Barker a benign glance. "My grandfather is stone deaf, with a sorrowful disposition. He lost his wife during the Interregnum – accused of witchery by the powers that be…"

Pepys froze mid-mouthful. "My sister suffered the same ordeal, and was saved only by Jacob and Abigail's astute attention."

Evelyn's eyes widened. "I see! So that is an inquisitor's work. How marvellous. My dear grandmother, alas could not be saved. After her death, Barnaby here abandoned his garden and lost all his mirth - he was once a fine plantsman, like myself."

With that, Evelyn launched into a series of dreary tales concerning the effect of the recent cold weather on his collection of rare plants.

Jacob, for one, found his mind wandering.

The previous Christmastide had been a miserable time for him, spent at his house on Strand Lane following the death of his father earlier that year. Shunned by his mother, Honoria, he had dined alone, warming himself by the fire deep into the night.

It had been cold then, he recalled, yet this December felt colder still. Despite Mr Pepys's walls being layered with tapestries and a fire going - a lengthy Yule log glowing at its heart - the dinner guests all wore coats, and the gentlemen their periwigs.

Suddenly, Jacob became aware that the room had fallen silent, and that all eyes were upon him. Flustered, he reached for his goblet, only to send it toppling. Thankfully, he had recently drained the contents. Coincidentally - or not - he felt a little light-headed.

"Well, Jacob?" Pepys asked.

"Very well, sir," he replied, "I am much obliged to you for enquiring."

Pepys groaned, theatrically slapping his forehead. "Mr Baines asked you a question, Jacob!"

Startled, the inquisitor turned to Baines, a solid yet nimble gentleman with flared nostrils and a cravat the colour of Abby's hair. He had deep-set, wandering eyes, and reminded Jacob of his angriest tutor.

"Forgive me," Jacob stammered. "I am an oaf."

That nobody contradicted him pained him somewhat.

"Do you have family, Mr Standish?" Baines repeated.

The inquisitor sighed. *I might as well not*, he thought to himself. "Aye, sir. Twin brothers who perished in the Dutch War, considerably braver than I. And three sisters." Coughing, he diverted the conversation back to Baines. "And you, sir?"

"Why, I, sir," the other man chortled, "have enough children that I can scarce keep count! At last reckoning, I believe there were three daughters and five…"

"Six," Evelyn corrected him.

Baines leaned back in his chair. "Thus my words are proven!" he said, eyeing his companion sidelong. "I have three daughters and *six* sons - a bountiful quiver, as Providence would have it."

Sitting up, he turned to Abby. "And you, Mistress Harcourt?"

She blinked, caught off guard by his civility. "Me?"

Pepys harrumphed. "Answer the gentleman."

"Why? Um… I fear not, sir."

Baines smiled faintly, studying her. "No brothers or sisters?"

Jacob, who knew that Abby's three brothers had all perished, gently touched her knee beneath the table.

"Nay, sir." Her voice cracked. "I wish there were."

Sensing the discomfort, Pepys rose and placed his hands on the table, "I think it time for a song!" he declared.

Having disappeared into his study, he returned with his recorder and began playing the tune to The Boar's Head, a carol with which they were all familiar (though Jacob found himself mouthing some of the words, and Barker wandered off to the privy mid-chorus).

The boar's head in hand bear I,
Bedeck'd with bays and rosemary.
And I pray you, my masters, be merry,
Quot estis in convivio.

Caput apri defero,
Reddens laudes Domino.

The boar's head, as I understand,
Is the rarest dish in all this land,
Which thus bedeck'd with a gay garland,
Let us servire cantico.

Caput apri defero,
Reddens laudes Domino.

Chapter Two

A Frost Fair

S now lay thick on the windowsills overlooking Seething Lane, and clung to the leaded framework of the diamond-shaped panes. Snowflakes the size of penny coins cavorted languidly through the glass.

Elizabeth Pepys and her maid had adorned the room with evergreens – holly, ivy and bay – which hung from the beams and framed the portraiture. Their mingling scents imbued the space with a welcome freshness, in stark contrast to its usual musty odour. The red berries glowed like scattered jewels, illuminated by flickering candlelight among the dark wood.

Baines pointed toward a garland of woven ivy tied with colourful ribbons. It hung above the doorway that led down to the kitchen. "Is that… *a kissing bough*, Mr Pepys?" he asked, his tone dripping with disdain.

Abby, who had spent more than two years in Pepys's household and knew him better than anyone present, spotted the tell-tale twitch of his cheek. He had complained to her about Evelyn's imposed guests only moments before their arrival.

"'Twas I who placed that there, Mr Baines," she cut in quickly. "If it offends you, I beg your forgiveness and offer my sincere apology."

Pepys reached gratefully for his wine.

Baines narrowed his eyes at Abby, thought better of chastising an innocent young woman, and barked, "So be it!"

St Olave's bell rang five times, and Jacob realised he might finally have begun to enjoy himself. His goblet had been refilled more times than he cared to count, and the buttons of his waistcoat now strained ominously.

He grinned to himself. It was his turn to introduce a topic of discourse, he decided, having heard quite enough about Mr Evelyn's garden. *I shall speak of my own endeavours!*

With that, he lurched to his feet. "Our first investigation for Mr Pepys," he announced, nodding to his mentor, "was to retrieve his stolen diaries, was it not, sir?"

Pepys's brown eyes flared. "I do not keep such a…"

"How marvellous, Sam!" Evelyn interjected, suddenly animated. "I, too, have kept a diary - since 1640, no less - when I was a student at Middle Temple. I find it invaluable to record my daily reflections and the blessings bestowed upon…"

But Jacob was not finished. "I confess, Mr Evelyn," he cut in, "that I misjudged the culprit entirely. I believed it to be Mr William Baxter, whose wife Mr Pepys had lain with…"

The atmosphere shifted in an instant, a chill descending on the room like frost upon a field.

"Jacob!" Abby snapped. Beside her, Pepys's cheeks flushed as red as his holly's berries.

Staring at the scowling faces around the table, Jacob swiped off his periwig and wrung it in his hands. "'Twas but a fabrication, I assure you - Mr Pepys's shrewd ruse to divert attention from the true culprit. A test of our suitability as his inquisitors."

"Aye," growled Pepys, "'twas indeed but a fabrication, Mr Standish, as well you know. I would never…"

"And I could never imagine you capable of such infidelity, sir," cut in Evelyn, smiling at Pepys. "An upstanding and honourable gentleman such as yourself."

Pepys dabbed his forehead with his napkin. "Aye, John. My dear wife, Elizabeth, means the world to me, and I would never betray her devotion," he blustered. "I… I…"

"Will the mistress be attending the Frost Fair?" Abby interjected. "I hear one is to be held upon the river."

Her employer eyed her gratefully. "I do hope so, Abigail, however… her constitution is at times fragile."

Jacob's eyes lit up. "Will there be a puppet play? I long to see one for myself. My sisters saw Pulcinella at Covent Garden, but I… was not permitted to attend."

"A man of simple pleasures," Pepys muttered, then louder added, "I believe fortune may favour you, Jacob. I witnessed the same performance, by the much admired Signor Napoli, whom I am told will indeed be attending the fair."

Jacob rubbed his hands in glee.

Baines piped up. "Rumour has it, the Italian will perform before His Majesty?"

Pepys dragged a hand across his wine-stained lips. "While 'tis true the King greatly admired Napoli's performance, and holds the puppeteer in rare esteem, I hear he finds the cold weather a bitter affront to his person, and may prefer to remain by his fireplace at court." He turned to Evelyn. "Will you be attending the Frost Fair, John?"

"Such massed expressions of frivolity are rather ungodly." Evelyn flicked a glance at his companions. "Are they not?"

Baines bit off a chunk of gingerbread, smiling inscrutably. Beside him, old Mr Barker had fallen asleep and was gently snoring.

"However," Evelyn continued, "having experienced the 1634 Frost Fair for myself, I must confess I found… moments of joy among its diversions."

"I myself did not witness the 1634 fair," Pepys replied, pausing. "Being but one year old."

Chuckling, Evelyn rose, poked his grandfather awake, and lofted his goblet. "Then let us drink to Mr Samuel Pepys - the finest host a gentleman could wish for!"

All stood and supped their drink, save for Pepys, who was already guzzling his.

"Mr Samuel Pepys!" came the chorus.

The host pushed himself to his feet. "I am obliged to you estimable gentlemen, and find I could not wish for heartier company!" Wobbling a little, he steadied himself with a hand. "Come! Let us drink to good English cheer! The Lord may grant salvation, but 'tis a full cup that grants contentment!" With that, he downed his own.

Only as he lowered it did he notice the offence Evelyn and Baines had taken - beer would never surpass the Lord in their attentions.

Catching one another's eye, they hid their amusement.

Despite its awkward moments, both had enjoyed the feast, which was a far cry from their previous Christmas-tides.

Chapter Three

St Stephen's Day

As consciousness gleefully whispered in Jacob's ear, his head began pounding like a blacksmith's hammer. All at once, the memories of the previous day's full goblets flooded back.

"Nay, nay, and thrice nay," he moaned.

In fairness, the occasion had ended on a high note, with dancing to Mr Pepys's drunkenly tuneless viol-playing. That is, he and Abby had danced. Mr Evelyn had politely tapped his foot while Barker snoozed, and Baines had descended into a wintry silence, broken only when Evelyn announced it was high time they took their leave.

Gingerly, Jacob opened his eyes. Seeing nothing but darkness, he wondered what time it was. *And where am I?* he wondered quite reasonably.

"How are you this morning, Jacob?" came the familiar, comforting voice.

Shifting, he realised he was cocooned in a blanket, fully clothed, on what felt like a stone floor. Against a wall, he could just make out an empty bed.

Illuminated in the doorway by the light of a candle she held, was Abby.

"What hour is this?" Jacob mumbled.

As if in reply, St Olave's bell began to toll.

Abby waited until the ninth chime rang out, and the silence returned, before replying. "'Tis nine of the clock, Jacob. On the day of St Stephen."

"Leave me be," he groaned, turning away from her reproachful gaze.

"Remember the Frost Fair!" she trilled.

Chapter Four

Fire & Snow

Cold, aching everywhere and parched, Jacob could not return to his slumber. The room in which he had slept never emerged from its gloom - he realised, after a while, that it had no windows. Compelled to haul himself to his feet, he made for the only source of light: the open doorway.

Emerging into the briefest of corridors, he found Abby next door, buttering bread in a kitchen area scarcely larger than his pantry. It was the only other room in the dwelling. There was a fire going, and at least it was warm.

Abby had lived on Seething Lane, in this converted naval storeroom gifted her by Pepys, for little over two months. Her kitchen's single, barred window let in scant light, and rats and mice would scamper over her as she lay in bed next door. Yet she called it home - gratefully, for it was the first she had ever owned.

"How are you?" she asked again, passing Jacob a thick slice of bread.

"How do you think?" he replied, staring at the dry sustenance in his hand. "Does Mr Pepys now despise me? Am I finished as his inquisitor?"

Abby rubbed his arm. "Nay, Jacob. 'Twas a slip of the tongue. Mr Pepys was guilty of the same, when he almost let slip our dreadful days at court."

Jacob nibbled tentatively at a crust. "Perhaps so, but will he see it the same? While I know him not well, he seems a man more inclined to apportion blame than to accept it."

Abby laughed. "You may be right. There's but one way to find out."

He stiffened. "Meet with him? I could not! It would be…"

"The wise choice?" Abby let her consoling hand drop. "If he bears you any ill will, then it's best to confront the matter. You'll survive, trust me."

Jacob exhaled deeply. "I do trust you, Abby, I do. You are…" He hesitated. "You are the most witty, clever and trustworthy friend a man could wish for, yet I…"

"Am a moonling," she finished for him, grinning. Then a thought struck her. "By the by, yesterday, when you told Mr Baines of your brothers, James and Robert…"

He nodded.

"…You told him they were braver than you."

"Aye. Since 'tis a fact."

"Nay, Jacob. Your reticence frustrates me. I've lost count of your acts of daring since becoming an inquisitor. Your heart beats with courage."

Studying his face, those doleful hazel eyes and down-turned lips, she saw he was not convinced. "Eat up," she said. "We leave soon."

As it transpired, Jacob had little to fear. When Pepys greeted them at his doorway, he appeared mired in the same malaise as his young inquisitor. Clad in layers - shirt, waistcoat, coat, all in the finest materials - and with his hands tucked inside a fur muff, he shook his head wearily as he donned his hat.

"How are you, sir?" Abby asked.

Pepys cleared his throat, pulled his coat tighter and looked up at the sky. It was cloudless and brilliant blue.

Yesterday's snowfall had deposited several inches of powder, with some drifts deep enough to reach a gentle-man's knee. Breath moved in clouds, and the air felt raw and insistent, like a graze.

Jacob, sullen and nervy, stamped his feet in his leather boots. Though he was dressed similarly to Pepys in layers, his unfashionable woollen garments were a far cry from his mentor's felt, fur and silk.

One of Abby's favourite privileges in her new role as inquisitor was the freedom to borrow Mistress Pepys's clothing – albeit under Elizabeth's watchful eye. She had discovered a newfound delight in dressing up and took every opportunity to indulge it.

Her own layers – chemise, bodice, petticoats, coat and cloak – were so plentiful, she felt a tad constricted; better that, she decided, than to freeze. Still she eyed Pepys's muff enviously, conscious of the thin leather of her borrowed gloves. Elizabeth had declined to lend hers, citing it as a precious gift from her husband, imported from France.

"Where to?" Abby asked.

The two men stared at their feet, devoid of impetus.

"I heard the Frost Fair may open today," she added hopefully.

Pepys brushed a light dusting of snow off his breeches. "Aye, Mr Evelyn spoke of the same ere he departed," Pepys replied, his fogged mind evident in his tone. "I am eager to see it for myself, Abigail."

"Sir?" Jacob ventured.

In the manner of a schoolmaster, Pepys turned his gaze on him. "I do not wish to hear a word from you, Mr Standish. Betray my confidence once again, and we shall part company – mark my words."

Jacob shifted uneasily as Pepys continued, "'Tis fortunate for you that I myself almost made a similar blunder. I confess, I found myself speaking merely to fill the awful silences, which may in some way excuse your indiscretion. I would sooner spend a night in Bedlam than another with Mr Evelyn's dour companions."

Rubbing his face vigorously with his muff, he strode towards the gate of the naval estate.

"Good day, Mr Pepys. Abigail. Mr Standish," the old porter, Walter Grenville, greeted the party as they reached his lodge. "Cold, ain't it?" he added, opening the gate.

Abby smiled at Grenville, while the men walked wordlessly past. Inside his wooden hut, she noticed a foot stove: a wooden box containing a metal pan of glowing coals. "You must be frozen, you poor man," she said, taking the porter's ungloved hand and rubbing it between hers. The pair had become friendly during Abby's many errands in and out of Pepys's property; though decades apart in age, they had bonded over a shared subservience.

"Leave that fellow alone!" Pepys snapped.

The old man winked at Abby, and she noticed tiny icicles on his bushy grey eyebrows.

"Stay warm," she bade him, following the others.

Raising his eyes, Grenville tutted quietly to himself and retreated to his inhospitable den.

The roofs and ledges of the buildings on either side of Seething Lane lay buried beneath an undulating cushion of snow. Thick black smoke billowed from the many tall chimneys, while warm, golden light glowed softly in the windows. Footsteps fell with a muffled crunch; even the dogs had ceased their irksome chatter.

London had fallen silent, and it felt like a blessed relief.

As the three figures reached the bottom of Seething Lane and turned right along Tower Street, a sight confronted them that caused them to draw a collective breath.

Each had become accustomed to the desolate panorama of London after the September fire: the stooped shapes of distraught Londoners picking through the flattened, blackened rubble; the plumes of smoke rising from persistent, isolated fires; the harsh, echoing din of demolition and rebuilding.

Now white, as far as the eye could see. A brilliant white that hurt the eyes.

It felt like the work of God, a soft blanket of calm to heal the stricken city.

Where men had lately sought out their burnt belongings, children now played, cavorting gaily and throwing snowballs.

"Oh my," gasped Abby.

The three of them lingered, gazing out over their city's delicately shrouded remnants, each lost in their own thoughts.

A sliver of the Thames was just visible in the distance, beyond London Bridge, now shorn of buildings and flattened on the northern end. Below them, east of the bridge, Pepys and his inquisitors could make out the same river, sluggish yet flowing, with boats scattered about.

Jacob cupped his hands and blew into them. "Sir, the river flows…" He stopped abruptly, remembering Pepys's instruction to remain silent.

Pepys, however, seemed already to have forgotten. "Are you not aware that the Thames may freeze only west of the bridge?"

Jacob shook his head.

Pepys waved him on. "Come, we must walk beyond the bridge to find access to the ice – if indeed there is ice to be found."

They made their way through the snow, Abby kicking at drifts, laughing as the glittering spray showered her face. Pepys elaborated as they walked.

When London experienced a hard winter, he said, the Thames began to freeze. Ice blocks would form, hazardous – sometimes fatal – to watermen and their passengers. Most would pass beneath one of London Bridge's nineteen arches, yet, occasionally, one might become trapped on a wooden starling protecting the stonework.

If enough of these trapped blocks accumulated, as the water continued to freeze, the river's flow would be impeded and slowed. "On rare occasions, and if the cold persists for many days, the river west of the bridge may freeze thick with ice," said Pepys, "upon which men may walk and coaches, even, may travel."

"Fie," said Jacob, blinking in wonderment. "For what purpose?"

"For the purpose of entertainment, Mr Standish. Your precious puppet show! I have seen illustrations of the previous fair, in which barbers cut hair, men played nine pins, and London's innkeepers set up tents on the ice."

"Fie," said Jacob again, grinning to himself.

Chapter Five

The Wager

Beyond London Bridge, a stretch of the wide Thames more than a mile long - all the way to Whitehall - came fully into view.

The river had indeed iced over.

Abby squealed with delight and clapped her hands. Jacob stood open-mouthed; even the more naturally reserved Pepys shook his clasped hands together at his chest, beaming broadly. "Well, I never did," he said, marvelling at the sight.

The river, once filthy brown and teeming with craft, now resembled a giant's frozen pathway. Intermittent snowdrifts had built up along the banks, and vast cubes of ice had collided at the foot of the bridge, contorting and shattering into jagged shapes.

Across the river, the buildings and fields of Southwark, untouched by the fire, lay crowned with snow. It looked, Pepys and his inquisitors grimly mused, how their city should have.

Yet there was no sign of a frost fair.

Here and there, mostly further upriver towards Whitehall, dotted figures could be seen out on the ice. Most seemed to tread warily - and wisely so, since darker patches on the surface hinted at thin ice in certain areas.

For beneath that deceptively solid sheath, the river flowed with its customary vigour, and woe betide any unfortunate who broke through.

They would be swept to their maker.

A hackney coach trundled past the trio as they continued along Thames Street, parallel to the river. None was tempted to take such a ride when travelling on foot, taking in the unique vista, felt so much more invigorating.

"Where are we heading, sir?" Jacob asked Pepys, enjoying the cloud of steam that billowed from his mouth as he did so.

"To Blackfriars," Pepys replied, puffing. "There appears to be a gathering."

Some half a mile ahead, near where the River Fleet met the Thames, a crowd had assembled.

Jacob was about to respond when a snowball took his hat off, followed by a chorus of childish giggles. The flushed faces of three young boys appeared over a bank of snow, their hands furiously compacting fresh ammunition to lob at the inquisitor.

"Cheeky young upstarts!" Jacob exclaimed, bending down to return their fire.

Abby joined in and was collecting her own snow when Pepys's voice stopped her in mid-scoop. "You are not children," he snapped. "You are my inquisitors."

Abby looked at Jacob, hatless and ruddy-faced, with a snowball in each hand like an overgrown schoolboy, and both burst into laughter.

At Blackfriars, several dozen Londoners had gathered around a gleaming black coach with red detailing, tethered to six snorting horses. Its owner, a bumptious-looking fellow with a voice to match, was arguing with a more shabbily-dressed man wearing a cocked cap, with narrowed eyes and a peg leg.

"I am not asking for fares; I request a wager!" the owner bellowed. "If I can drive my carriage across the river, then…"

The other man cut him off, jabbing a finger into his puffed-up chest. "This is my river," he snarled, then caught himself, turning to the men crowded behind him. "Nay, this is our river!"

A rough cheer rose from the gathered men.

"For we, sir, are the Thames watermen," he went on. "And this foul ice deprives us of our livelihoods."

Abby noticed Pepys open his mouth to protest, and was glad when he closed it.

It had not occurred to her that a frost fair, which promised such gaiety and entertainment, also threatened a darker side.

How will the watermen feed their families, she wondered, *when the river is emptied of their wherries?*

As she did so, her gaze drifted to a bare, gnarled tree, split in two as if by lightning. That damage had come not from the sky, she realised, but from the bitter, biting cold.

"What is your name, waterman?" the coach-owner asked, slapping one of his horses on the rump, causing it to whinny.

The waterman barely nodded his head. "I am Duke Hobbes, Master of the Company of Watermen and Lightermen. Who am I addressing?"

The other man bowed, all the while eyeing Hobbes. "I own the warehouse yonder," he replied, pointing across the river to an expansive wooden property set behind Paris Garden Stairs. "I am Henry Compton, sir, wine merchant, and I offer you my assistance."

Hobbes spat, to rumbles of assent from his gathered colleagues. "How so?"

"If my coach and six heavy horses can make it from this bank to the far bank, then the ice will bear any load. London may once again host a frost fair, as it has done in the past, and you and your Company can pitch tents and charge a fee for their usage."

Hobbes rubbed his stubbly chin. "And why would you take that risk?"

"Because, sir, I am drunk!" Compton declared, throwing open his arms.

Hats flew in the air as a great cheer rose from the crowd.

Abby nudged Jacob. "This should be interesting."

A ramp was constructed using timber purloined from silenced yards nearby, which ran from the bank down to the ice. All the while, Compton collected wagers from onlookers.

Although popular opinion suggested he would plunge to his doom through the ice, he did not seem in the least bit perturbed.

By the time the preparations were finished, the crowd of spectators had more than doubled in size. Abby, sheltering from the icy breeze in the lee of Pepys and Jacob, noticed so many others ill-equipped for the weather. There were children dressed in little more than rags, their feet bare in the snow, shivering yet apparently excited to witness the coming spectacle.

Henry Compton sat high up at the front of his coach, whip in hand, while his horses gazed down at the ice, shaking their heads. Even the beasts, it seemed, were aware of his folly.

A hush descended.

Slugging from a silver flask with a flourish, Compton cracked his whip. "Onward, my beauties!" he bellowed. "Our prize awaits us!"

The horses stepped warily forward, the two leaders' front hooves contacting the ice.

The crowd held its breath as, with a few more steps, the front wheels of the coach rolled off the ramp and onto the solid Thames surface. The ice groaned and a crack travelled along its very edge, to onlookers' gasps - yet Compton only urged his beasts onward.

Jacob felt Abby take his hand and clutch it so tightly it hurt. He was glad of the meagre warmth.

As the rear wheels of the coach left the ramp, spectators began to cheer. The gathered watermen, sensing opportunity, began chanting: "Frost fair! Frost fair!"

It was strange to see this vast wagon and its bridled horses, seemingly walking on water.

Compton turned to address the crowd. "What did I tell you!"

As he turned back, his lead horse slipped, its front hoof skating forward, lurching the beast sideways and downwards, pulling its neighbour with it. The horses behind struggled to maintain their balance, hooves scraping against the ice in panicked chaos, and the coach began to arc sideways.

Cries of horror rose from the onlookers, louder even than the drunken wine merchant's cackling laughter.

He appeared to be enjoying himself!

The horses managed to right themselves, hauling their burden back on course, and Pepys bent down to mutter in Abby's ear, "He is a braver man than I. And decidedly more foolhardy."

Children began streaming onto the ice in the coach's wake, cavorting happily, while petrified parents called them back. Some slipped and fell, only to pick themselves up and careen, slipping and sliding, after the departing Compton.

All watched as this curious menagerie grew smaller and smaller, until it reached the far bank 300 yards away, safely and in one piece. There, the tiny figure of Henry Compton stood on his seat, arms aloft, his faint cries of triumph carried on a chill wind.

Jumping up and down as one tight rabble, the watermen once again found their voices, and were joined by their fellow Londoners. Abby and Jacob found themselves swept along by joyous sentiment; even Mr Pepys quelled his dignity for long enough to add to the swelling chorus.

"Frost fair! Frost fair!"

Over the commotion, the Master of the Company of Watermen and Lightermen turned to his colleagues and bellowed, "We build tonight!"

A great cheer rose, echoing across the barren river.

Chapter Six

Lost Brothers

Jacob could not face another night sleeping on Abby's floor, so the inquisitors repaired to his grand townhouse on Strand Lane. It would be closer to the action, they decided, considerably more restful, and, most importantly, warmer.

No matter how many layers they wore, the winter cold gnawed right through them.

Since they had dined at Mr Pepys's on Christmas Day, there were no leftovers for supper. Instead, Jacob's reinstated maid - he had foolishly dismissed the woman, deeming himself unworthy of servants - baked them a pie filled with boar and venison, garnished with leeks, carrots, turnip and cabbage. Afterwards, they nibbled contentedly on gingerbread.

"How far we have come, Jacob," Abby mused, as they sat before the fire in his parlour.

Jacob patted his bloated stomach. "Aye, yet I fear I could go no further."

Abby smiled. It was not merely their status she had referred to; she felt so comfortable in his company now, as if she had known him all her life - as if he were a brother.

She sensed that Jacob felt the same, but he was not one to reveal his deepest emotions.

Emboldened by her tankard of sack, she decided to brooch their relationship, and wondered how best to raise the subject. Too clumsily, and he would retreat into his stiff manners.

Her eyes scanned the family portraits around the dark-wood walls. There, Jacob's three sisters - Elizabeth, Margaret and Anne - the first two successfully married-off, and Anne… Abby could barely countenance the thought of the King's young mistress after their trials at court.

Ahead of her, beside the family coat of arms above the stone fireplace, were depicted Jacob's parents, the late Sir Miles and Lady Honoria Standish. The same Lady Honoria who had banished him here from the family estate in Greenwich. Jacob, the outcast.

And there, his twin brothers, James and Robert, earnestly captured in their tight blue doublets, clutching hourglasses. Now dead. They had perished together, inseparable as they were, during the Dutch War the previous year, not long before their father had succumbed to a mysterious illness.

"Do you miss your brothers?" Abby asked.

He exhaled.

The fire crackled as the harsh squawk of a gull standing on the chimney echoed down the flue.

"Do you miss…" she persisted.

Jacob cut her off. "Aye, Abigail. I miss them. They were my brothers."

"Were you close?" She knew they were not, but could not stop herself asking.

Her cosy *tête-à-tête* was not going well.

Jacob took a gulp of his own sack. Even without looking, she could sense his knitted brow.

"I miss my brothers," she said, filling the silence. "I miss them very much."

Realising that his foot was tapping furiously on the oak floor, Jacob clutched at his knee to still it. Abby's three brothers were gone, he knew. She had told him of her mother dying in childbirth, and the baby, John, not surviving. It occurred to him that he had never asked the names of the other two.

"William, John and Henry," she said quietly, as if reading his mind.

"Were you close?"

For a good while, no one spoke.

Chapter Seven

Aulay Cussell

*I*n 1625, King Charles I passed the Act of Revocation, aimed at reclaiming swathes of Scottish land granted away during the previous century. It struck fear into the hearts of local landowners, who had long relied on royal favour to secure their holdings.

One such landowner was Ewan Cussell of Stirling. His estate, a few hundred acres of field, pasture and woodland, had once belonged to the Catholic Church, before being seized and redistributed during the Scottish Reformation. It was modest, but it sufficed. Tenant farmers worked the land, while the family lived in a stone cottage overlooking the valley.

Now, for the first time in generations, his right to it was in question.

Ewan had inherited the estate from his father, Alexander, as had his father before him.

Alexander Cussell, a minor courtier, had fought for King James VI at the Battle of Glenlivet. In return for his loyalty, *so he claimed, he had been granted a fertile stretch of land north of London, in High Barnet.*

He had never offered proof. A letter from King James was spoken of, but never seen. Yet Ewan believed him absolutely.

"My father wid ne'er invent such a thing," he assured his wife, Morag.

"Then where's the house, the tenants, the rent, that shid have fed us long ago?" she would counter.

"D'ye no see, Morag? They're oors tae claim!"

Aulay Cussell was four years old when, in the summer of 1626, his father left Stirling for London to do just that, taking his family with him. His sister, Ailsa, was ten.

They took their mule, Muckle, and a small two-wheeled cart to carry their belongings. If they were lucky, the children were allowed to hitch a ride when they grew tired, and his father would often carry Aulay on his back.

It would be a demanding, treacherous journey - more than 400 miles - with no stagecoaches covering the route. But once Ewan had made up his mind, what choice did they have?

Rival landowners had begun circling the Cussell estate, eager to take advantage of the Crown's sudden interest in old feudal rights. Ewan chose exile over submission, convinced that a more prosperous life awaited them outside London.

"We shall have what we are owed, eh, Aulay?" he said, playfully punching his son.

Aulay worshipped the man, would have followed him to the edge of the world.

Morag was growing less enamoured.

They left in the dead of night, telling no one. At Ewan's insistence, there would be no farewells, no explanations – he would not face the tenants' uproar when they woke to find the Cussells gone.

To Aulay and Ailsa, it felt tantalising. The sky was a vast canvas of starlight, and all around, the world lay sleeping.

Morag had packed only the essentials, since it was vital to travel light. Muckle, the mule, was old, and she could only pray the poor beast would last the journey. The prospect of pulling the cart by hand did not bear considering.

They dressed in rough farming clothes, shoddy enough to deter robbers. At his belt, Ewan carried a purse of copper coins, ready to hand over with feigned protestations should they be held up. The real money – more than ten pounds in silver, enough to last weeks in London – was hidden in a small bag inside Muckle's feed sack.

As they set out, Ewan and Morag led the mule, while the children skipped along behind. She had packed spare shoes, knowing they would be needed.

The dirt tracks toward Edinburgh passed through green lowlands.

Aulay clambered onto the cart and dug out a portion of smoked fish. "When will we be in London?" he asked, chewing on the salty meat.

No one answered.

By the sixth day, they reached Berwick-upon-Tweed, crossing into England. An inn by the stone bridge over the river offered them their first real bed.

After sleeping in hedgerows when the weather was kind, or church porches when the heavens opened, a straw mattress felt like luxury. Their feet were blistered in unforgiving leather shoes, their skin raw from the sun, and they were bitten all over by the persistent midges and blackflies.

If the adventure had begun to wear thin, nobody said so.

The next few days were miserable. They trudged over rough moorland, hauling the cart through deep ruts, while the rain never ceased. It weighed down their woollen clothing, sat in their shoes, soaked their belongings and chilled them through.

One night, Ewan urged them past a remote alehouse, determined to press on, but the weather turned on them. With no shelter, they slept in the open, huddled beneath dripping cloaks.

Little Aulay stuffed his fingers in his ears as his parents rowed, sharing shelter with Ailsa, who coughed and sneezed all night.

By the time they dragged themselves into Newcastle, they were sodden, bedraggled and exhausted. Morag insisted on paying for a room. Ailsa, in particular, was suffering – her freckled face puffy and crimson, fever burning her brow. A plague had blighted England that year, and the parents hid their concerns.

While Morag tended to Ailsa, Ewan took Aulay down to the River Tyne.

Newcastle was England's chief coal port, supplying London by sea along the east coast. The air reeked of smoke and the river was black with grime. Aulay, who had never seen anything like it, was mesmerised.

Men were everywhere – tough men, tougher even than his father – their faces streaked with coal dust, their hands black as midnight. They loaded barges with practised ease, readying them for the journey downriver, where vast colliers waited to carry their cargo to the capital.

Edging forward, drawn by the sheer energy and clamour of it all, Aulay's foot slipped on the dock's edge, slick with dust.

A hand seized his collar, hauling him back. "Yer father'll be fishing y'outta the Tyne, bonny lad," his rescuer chuckled, before thrusting a lump of coal into his palm. "Black gold, that is," he said. "Keep it."

Ailsa was so weak the next morning that she had to ride in the cart. The extra weight slowed their already painfully slow progress, and Muckle, reduced to a hobble, protested in fits and snorts.

The road, following dirt tracks, grew hilly. The climbs were tortuous, the descents, merciful. As they neared farmland on a detour into York, planning for an inn, Muckle simply lay down and never rose again.

Morag hammered her fists into the old beast's rump as she harangued her husband. "We've a sick child, barely enough food, a wee bairn and a cart wi' nae mule. Whit're we gonna do? Are you gonna pull the thing the rest o' the way, Ewan Cussell?"

And pull it, he did, through the remaining miles into York, where he sold it for a few shillings. The buyer, a grain merchant with a crooked smile, smelled his desperation.

"Let's turn back," Morag pleaded.

"We cannae," her husband replied bluntly. "We've come halfway."

They had no choice but to stay in York. With Ailsa too weak to walk and the cart gone, they could not carry both their belongings and a stricken child.

On the third day, miraculously, Ailsa's fever broke. She sat up, took food, and the sheen on her brow faded. Her dulled green eyes brightened.

By the fifth day, they could continue. But their funds were depleted, and with the cart gone, Ewan and Morag had to sell some provisions and lash what was left to their backs.

The remainder of the journey, via Lincoln and Stamford, following the ancient Roman Ermine Street, should have taken three weeks. It took almost twice that.

The monotony of putting one foot in front of the other, day after day, when their feet, legs, backs and minds craved rest, became a grim battle.

Ewan carried Aulay in his arms whenever he could, but he could not endure it for long.

The child rarely grumbled, even if his skip had noticeably slowed.

At a market in Grantham, as Morag haggled for a few bread rolls, Aulay drifted away between the villagers, small enough to go unnoticed. When he returned, he pressed something metal into her hand.

She glanced down – a silver sixpence.

Her eyes bored into his; he shrugged, a picture of innocence beneath a thatch of bright orange hair.

As she handed the coin to the baker, Aulay smirked to himself.

But cruel fate had not finished with the Cussells of Stirling.

Even as they approached London's outskirts, just two days from their destination, the worst happened.

They were nearing Baldock, a market town in Hertfordshire. The road cut through open heathland, offering little shelter but plenty of hiding places among the gorse and high bushes.

It was late afternoon, the sun slipping behind thick grey clouds. A damp chill hung in the air, and the road was quiet – almost too quiet. The usual trickle of carts and travellers had thinned; even the birdsong had faded.

Morag felt it first – the prickling sense of being watched.

Then, out of the brush, they came.

Two men on horseback, their faces wrapped in kerchiefs, pistols raised in gloved hands.

"Coin!" the leader barked, guiding his horse to block their path. The second man circled behind, cutting off any hope of escape, though, in truth, they lacked the strength to flee.

Ewan stepped forward, placing himself between his family and the robbers. "We've nought worth robbing," he said.

The leader's eyes flicked to Aulay and Ailsa, to their threadbare clothes, and the bundles lashed to Morag's back. "Let me be the judge of that," he said, dismounting.

He strode up to Morag, while his accomplice glanced nervously around. When he grabbed at her baggage, she refused to let go, and he yanked her to the ground.

Ewan lunged, fists swinging, catching the man in the jaw and sending him staggering back, cursing.

Aulay heard the crack before he saw the pistol move.

Ewan staggered, then sank to his knees.

Morag screamed.

All eyes turned to the mounted robber, smoke curling from his pistol.

The leader's gaze was panicked – they had not planned to kill a man.

All was deathly silent as, with trembling hands, he rifled Ewan's clothing. Snatching the penny-purse from his belt, he held it aloft for his accomplice to see.

Then they were gone, galloping back into the gorse.

Ewan Cussell, who had dragged his family across the country on the hopes of a dream, would never see London.

Chapter Eight

To the Thames

Abby, who had once risen before dawn as Pepys's maidservant, had quickly grown accustomed to a more leisurely start since her promotion to inquisitor.

The bedding at Jacob's was particularly soft, a far cry from her coarse wool of yore, and on the morning of the 27th, she drifted in and out of sleep, even as the chimes of the local church bells increased in number. Not even the prospect of the Frost Fair could part her from those soft Rennes linen sheets.

"Rise and shine!"

Jacob's exhortation, punctuated by the *clang-clang-clang* of spoon on pan, woke her with a jolt.

Grumbling incoherently, she felt his hand shake her shoulder.

"'Tis the first morning of the Thames Frost Fair," he said, "and I am eager to see it."

Turning over, she was greeted by his boyish grin, hazel eyes twinkling beneath those extensive brows.

"'Tis eight of the clock!" he added, his breath somewhat pungent at close quarters.

Shaking her head, she managed a thin smile, one eye open. "Await me downstairs."

"Will you…?"

"Nay, Jacob, I won't be long!"

A young woman's tumble of layers was hardly conducive to swift dressing, but she did her best to keep her word. Jacob, meanwhile, sat drumming his fingers impatiently.

Leaving his residence, they turned right onto The Strand and made their way towards Temple Bar, the historic gateway dividing Westminster from the City of London. Westminster had largely escaped the fire's destruction, but beyond the grand arch, the cityscape altered abruptly. Barely a hundred yards ahead, the buildings simply ceased to be.

It felt like stepping from one world into another: from magnificence into desolation.

Around them, the snow-crusted halls, libraries and chapels of the Inns of Court stood in quiet defiance; ahead, a whitewashed wasteland.

Taking Middle Temple Lane down towards the river, they found reassurance in the tall buildings flanking them. London had not entirely succumbed to the flames and would, in time, rise from the rubble to flourish again.

But for now, they had the fair. That, surely, would gladden any weary heart.

And suddenly, there it was, stretching out before them – a sight that stopped Abby and Jacob in their tracks.

Two rows of canvas booths were rising across the width of the river, forming a street that stretched from Temple Stairs below them in the direction of Barge House in Southwark. The watermen, having worked through the night, had built the booths halfway across, but beyond that, the street remained unfinished. In the distance, men toiled on the ice, securing the remainder of the makeshift stalls. Soon, the thoroughfare would span the full width of the Thames.

Where only yesterday the ice had been all but barren, now it thronged with people, desperate to experience even this incomplete fair. Few among them would have been alive for the last great Frost Fair of 1634–35.

More were gathering at the top of Temple Stairs, preparing to take their first steps onto the frozen Thames, and they joined them. The huddled bodies proved a welcome buffer against the fierce east wind that had struck them upon emerging from Middle Temple Lane.

Overhead, a blanket of cloud threatened fresh snow.

"What shall we do first?" Jacob asked with childlike glee, ignoring a hunch-backed old woman who was tugging at his sleeve, offering to tell his fortune.

Abby, who had forgotten her gloves in the morning's haste, rubbed her numbed hands briskly. "I've never seen you so joyful, Jacob. Your smile suits you."

"Tell your fortune, good sir," the old woman persisted, still clinging to his coat.

Irritably, Jacob pushed her hand aside. "Besides puppetry, what entertainment does a frost fair offer?" he asked Abby. "I confess I know not where to start."

It occurred to Abby that she was equally inexperienced in such matters. Mr Pepys had shown her a woodcut of the last fair, but that was some while ago, and she strained to recall its details. "There was a barber," she managed.

Jacob gazed down at her askance. "A *barber*? I would not consider the cutting of hair to be... entertaining."

"Danger awaits you, sir! Mortal danger."

It was the old woman again.

Jacob could ignore her no longer, and he turned to face her. She was half his size, wrapped in a black shawl, her face lined with deep furrows.

"What say you, old hag?" he asked.

Her chapped blue lips curled. "The gentleman heard my warning - but does he heed it?"

"Ignore her, Jacob," Abby said.

"Master Jacob, is it?" the old woman said, seizing his hand and turning it palm up.

Shaken, he did not pull away.

"Oh dear," the old woman murmured after a moment's inspection. "'Tis worse than I feared."

Abby stepped between them. "Leave him be," she said. "You'll get no money from us."

"How so?" Jacob demanded, oblivious to her intervention. "What is worse than you feared?"

Abby had no choice but to bundle the old woman away, pushing her back into the crowd.

"Beware, Master Jacob!" the fortune teller called over her shoulder. "Beware the man with the crooked nose!"

With that, she was gone, swallowed by the throng.

"What did she mean?" Jacob asked.

Tucking her arm into his, Abby shivered. "She's but a charlatan. Ignore her."

A set of wide wooden stairs led down to the river, branching into two to allow the crowd to disperse. As Abby and Jacob began their descent, the heavy clouds overhead loosened their burden, distracting him from the fortune teller's warning. Large, soft flakes of snow swirled like dervishes in the wind, whipping into their faces, stinging, yet invigorating.

Around them, voices rose in wonder; some reached up to catch the flakes, others tasting them on their tongues.

The last time London last seen such a shower, it had been of ash, drifting from the fire. Now, the people seemed bound together in a barely contained euphoria.

At the lowest stair, Abby paused to watch as Jacob took his first, tentative steps onto the ice.

Though he slid a little, hastily throwing out his arms for balance, he managed to remain upright. Puzzled as to why she had not followed, he turned. "What is it?" he asked.

"You didn't fall."

"Did you expect that I would?"

Abby laughed. "Jacob, you're the clumsiest man I've ever met!"

The crowd behind her began growing impatient. Jacob stepped forward and offered his hand. She placed one foot, then the other, onto the sheer Thames surface, let out a yelp, and toppled backwards as her legs flew out and upwards.

Instinctively, Jacob caught her before she hit the ground, hoisting her aloft. She dangled in his grip, feet flailing, while impatient Londoners streamed past on either side. Several made it barely a few yards before sprawling flat on their faces. Yet Jacob, still holding her aloft, stood firm.

Her eyes, for once level with his, shot him a look. "You're a strange fellow, Jacob Standish."

"Good morrow, Mr Standish."

The unexpected greeting made Jacob start, and his grip slackened just enough for Abby to drop to the ice. She landed with an audible *thump* on her backside. There she sat, dazed, as a hand reached down to aid her.

"And good morrow to you, Mistress Harcourt," said John Evelyn, hauling her upright.

On either side of Evelyn stood his erstwhile dinner companions, Arthur Baines and Barnaby Barker, the latter tiny and hunched. The three had dressed for the conditions - thick periwigs, stout leather gloves and boots, cravats - and each carried a cane to steady themselves on the ice.

Jacob eyed them enviously. They wore their gentlemen's accoutrements with such ease, while he merely played the part. Baines stood with his feet splayed, upright and assured, gloved hands draped over the head of his cane, smiling benignly.

He knows, thought Jacob, tugging at his own, rather threadbare periwig.

Profoundly unsteady, Abby clung to her fellow inquisitor, to Barker's evident disapproval.

"No Mr Pepys?" Evelyn asked.

"Nay, sir," Jacob replied. "He attends to naval business, but assured us he would meet us here for dinner." He glanced about, wondering at their slim chances of spotting one another amid such crowds.

Baines coughed pointedly.

"Well, we must away…" Evelyn began.

But Abby cut him off. "You've visited a frost fair before, sir?"

"I have indeed."

"What entertainment is here?" Jacob asked.

Evelyn looked him up and down. "Why, Mr Standish, you shall find men sliding on skates, bull-baiting, horse and coach races, puppet plays and interludes, cooks, tippling…"

Jacob was about to express his delight when Evelyn's expression darkened.

"…And other such lewd happenstances," he added. "A frost fair seems to me a Bacchanalian triumph, an unholy carnival on the water. This perishing cold casts a severe judgment upon the land." He paused the tirade, then added as an afterthought, "I fear my poor rosemary and myrtle will have perished."

With that, he shook his head and made for the street of booths. Baines growled as he and Barker followed in his wake.

Abby motioned for Jacob to lean close to her and whispered in his ear, "Yet still he visits."

Chapter Nine

On Thin Ice

At the head of the street of booths stood a sign:

TEMPLE STREET

Further signs hung perpendicular to certain establish-ments along the street. Among them, The Duke of York's Coffee House, The Roast Beef Booth and The Horn Tav-ern Booth. It was as if city itself had been transferred to the ice. How the tradesmen who had lost their businesses in the fire would welcome the chance to revive their custom, however briefly.

Jacob discovered the fair's drawback when he hastened to the Duke of York's. Yearning for a cup of coffee - a taste he had lately acquired, enjoying its air of sophistica-tion - he was dismayed when the owner quoted a price of thruppence, rather than the customary penny.

"That, sir, is an outrage!" he told the owner. "I shall not pay it!"

The owner bowed politely. "Good sir, I am bound to pay the watermen's tariff for the use of this booth, which, I trust, warrants my price." He gestured around the tent, where Londoners huddled over their coffees, drawing warmth from the rising steam. "Plenty, as you can see, agree."

"Hmph!" harrumphed Jacob, gazing at the contented faces. How dearly he wished to sup the same heady brew, to feel its heat invigorate his insides. "I shall not pay it!" he repeated for good measure.

"Two coffees, if you please," he heard Abby ask.

"I thought you did not care for the drink," Jacob huffed as they took shelter in a corner of the temporary coffee house, gratefully reviving their frigid hands on hot bowls.

"I don't," Abby replied. "But I'm cold, and the coffee is warm."

When she nudged him playfully, he merely lofted his chin.

"And how do you afford this blackguard's extortionate prices?" he persisted.

"Mr Pepys finally paid me. My new inquisitor's wage."

Glancing around to ensure no prying eyes, she extracted a cloth pouch from her satchel and loosened the drawstring, allowing Jacob to peek inside.

He spared it barely a glance. "I see only silver and copper."

With a tut, she closed the pouch and tossed it back into her bag. "'Tis easy for you to say, with your golden guineas galore. As Mr Pepys's maid, I earned a shilling a week. As his inquisitor," she lowered her voice, "I am paid one half-crown."

When Jacob expressed only indifference, she sighed and turned her attention elsewhere.

"Sailcloth," she said, running a hand along the tent's fabric. Then, tracing the wooden frame, added, "And oars, lashed together. The watermen are more ingenious than we give them credit."

Jacob, recalling Pepys's favoured watermen - the insolent Kilgore brothers, who took great pleasure in mocking his stature - promptly changed the subject. "Where shall we visit next? I am eager to see one of these puppet plays. And the coach races Mr Evelyn mentioned - on the ice! Can it be true?"

His inner youth was surfacing again.

"Shall we find out?" Tossing back the last of her coffee, Abby gagged on the coarse dregs.

Many of the traders were still setting up their booths. The toy seller was arranging spinning tops and knucklebones on his wooden shelves; the Lottery Booth owner, a rotund fellow with bulging eyes like a spaniel's, was awaiting banners in preparation for his first draw; two men staggered past, hauling a vast beam of timber, its destination unknown.

To his dismay, Jacob found that one of the few traders fully operational was the barber.

"Perhaps he could trim your periwig?" Abby teased.

The Horn Tavern, they discovered, had been supplanted from Fleet Street to the frozen Thames, as The Horn Tavern Booth. Snug inside, warmed by a flaming brazier and one another's bodies, guests were already gathered, supping on ales and smoking their pipes.

Abby dragged Jacob away from its easy indulgences, not wishing to be trapped among gaggles of boorish drinkers.

At length, they reached the end of the parallel rows of completed booths and found themselves surrounded by stacked oars, canvas and ropes. Watermen, some stripped to their waists, such was their toil, were continuing the construction of Temple Street, overseen by the peg-legged Duke Hobbes - the same man who had assumed charge of the previous day's daring wager.

The opposite bank at Southwark was still a good hundred yards away.

Hobbes's leg had been amputated below the knee. He hobbled apace on a wooden peg-leg, unaided by a crutch, relying on sheer strength and grit to maintain his balance. A cutlass lay slung across his chest in a leather baldric, suggesting he was not a man to be trifled with.

"Lively now, lads!" he cried, before turning to a group of four men discoursing some distance away. "And Carter…?"

A wiry, bare-chested young man among them stiffened. "Aye, sir?"

"Get them runners on them wherries, like I told yer!"

"Aye-aye, sir!" Carter called back, instantly setting off along the ice in a swift rhythm of sprints and slides. The watermen, it seemed, were at home on the Thames, whether it was solid or liquid.

Out of the corner of his eye, Jacob caught movement - the other three men were approaching fast, metal flashing at their heels.

"Skaters, Jacob," Abby pointed out, sensing his puzzlement.

Hobbes saw them, too, and began furiously waving his arms. "Get away from there, you lackwits! 'Tis thin ice!"

The lead skater cupped a hand to his ear. "What say you?" His accent was not of England.

"I said, that's thin ice!" Hobbes hollered. "You'll go through and drown, you…!"

Before he could finish, the skaters were upon him, turning sideways in unison. Their blades carved into the ice, sending up a shower of glittering shards. They wore long woollen cloaks and fur-lined gloves; each had a leather satchel slung across their shoulder.

Hobbes lurched forward and seized the leader by the scruff of his shirt. "Don't want no deaths on my river. Send the crowds away. Who are yer?"

"I am Dirk de Vries," the man replied, seemingly unperturbed by Hobbes's brutishness. He nodded toward a shorter man with a neat blond beard. "This is my friend, Hendrick van der Haagen."

"I am Maarten," the third man volunteered, waving almost apologetically. "Hendrick's brother."

"If there is thin ice," de Vries said, "why would you not place barriers around it?"

Hobbes shoved hard, sending de Vries flailing backward. He landed awkwardly on his elbow, cried out in pain, and began sliding toward the treacherous patch, clawing frantically at the ice to cease his progress.

When, at last, he came to a halt, the awful, deep snap of the cracking ice preceded the sight of it.

De Vries's bright blue eyes widened. His friends stood mute in horror. Jacob moved to help, but Abby seized his coat. "'Tis too perilous," she hissed.

A crack, some three feet long, ran jagged through the pale, frosted surface. For long seconds, de Vries sat up, rigid. Then, in an instant, he was on his feet, skating back toward his friends, terror stark on his windblown face.

Behind him, the ice groaned again, and the crack crept farther across the frozen surface.

De Vries pitched headlong into Hobbes – whether by accident or design, the inquisitors could not tell – sending him crashing backwards onto the ice. At once, Hobbes's fellow watermen swarmed around him, several hauling him to his feet.

"Madman!" the skater bellowed. "You could have killed me!"

Dazed, Hobbes tottered, braced by his comrades, before standing firm. Then, advancing, he unsheathed his cutlass, a wide sneer exposing blackened teeth.

"Dirk! Let's go!" Maarten urged, already pivoting on the heel of his skate.

Abby fancied she could see de Vries's mind racing and breathed a sigh of relief when he turned and sped away. The three skaters shot toward the south bank, their howls of indignation swallowed by the baying laughter of the watermen.

When finally the mirth subsided, Hobbes barked an order. "Somebody place a barrier round that thin ice!"

Chapter Ten

The Italian

"Would you consider Hobbes's nose to be crooked?" Jacob asked.

It took Abby a little while. "Jacob!" she said. "Tell me you don't believe the old fortune teller's words. Did our days in Brampton mean nought to you?"

In Brampton, where Pepys's parents and sister lived, they had encountered false accusations of witchery and the devious games of the witch-finder, Simon Hopkins.

"Well, I… I would not…" Jacob stammered.

"Forget the crooked nose," she told him bluntly.

"I don't like that waterman, Hobbes."

"Neither I," Abby replied distractedly. Her attention had been drawn to a dark-haired man out on the ice, some distance from Temple Street. He was setting up his own tent, vibrant in reds and yellows, beside a cart stacked with equipment.

"Come," she said, setting off to investigate.

The snow had stopped, leaving an inch-thick layer of powdery fluff atop the ice. Abby kicked at it and fell over.

When Jacob stooped to pick her up, she shook her head incredulously. "Show me your soles," she said.

"For why?"

"You must have pitch there. I can't believe you've not fallen."

Abby lifted his foot, as she might a horse's. His sturdy leather boots reached to mid-calf, double-soled and hob-nailed. "And the other." As expected, it was identical.

Grinning to herself, she wrenched his foot backward. With a shriek - a lady's shriek - he toppled to the ice, sending his hat and precious periwig tumbling.

"Abigail Harcourt!" he exclaimed, the left side of his face plastered in rime.

Shovelling up a handful of snow, he launched a snowball at her, missing by a furlong, just as hers struck him square on the forehead.

The first of several church bells echoed the chimes of two of the clock about the river. The dark-haired man had already attracted a crowd of onlookers as Abby and Jacob joined him.

He wore a rich-blue doublet and matching breeches, the doublet unbuttoned over a loose linen shirt. His long, wavy hair was tied back, and as he bent to work, a wooden crucifix on a leather thong slipped free, swinging like a ship's lantern in a storm.

Everybody seemed to notice. Mutters rippled through the crowd and sneers were exchanged. If there were Catholics among them, they were too afeared to make themselves known.

A large, elaborately decorated sign lay flat on the ice, identifying this curious figure. Painted on it, alongside a figure clad in white, wearing a long-nosed black half-mask, were the words:

Signor Napoli

Presents

The Famous Italian Puppet Play

By Royal Command

December 30. 1666

Jacob nudged Abby excitedly. "The puppet play!"
She beamed back.

Having created a framework of wooden poles lashed together, Signor Napoli began wrestling with the colourful canvas Abby had spied from a distance.

"Will nobody assist me?" he asked, his voice lilting with a foreign cadence.

Heads shook; a few tutted.

Only one man stepped forward: Jacob Standish.

Glancing with undisguised disdain at the others in the crowd, Napoli beckoned him forward. "Come! Come!

Quickly! You will assist the great Signor Napoli. You are most welcome, kind sir."

When Jacob reached him, he asked, "What is your name?"

Jacob, who had not anticipated becoming a player in the puppeteer's show, began fiddling with his periwig. "J…Jacob," he blurted out.

"Excellent!" declared Napoli, clapping his hands together. "Then you will assist me in lifting this canvas over the frame, J-Jacob!"

Several chuckled.

"'Tis just Jacob, sir," Jacob pointed out, head bowed.

Behind him, Abby cringed in sympathy.

"So be it!" declared Napoli. "Then you will assist me in lifting this canvas over the frame, just-Jacob-sir!"

"Nay, I meant…" Jacob began to protest, but his words were drowned out by howls of laughter. Only Abby declined to join in.

While Napoli lifted and manoeuvred the canvas with ease, Jacob found it awfully cumbersome. Losing his footing, he slammed chin-first onto the ice, and felt certain the puppeteer had caused his fall with a tug.

It did not matter to the crowd, whose hilarity only heightened.

When Jacob tumbled a second time, only to emerge head-first through a window cut into the front of the canvas, one woman fell over laughing.

Even Abby could not help herself, and had to turn away to hide her amusement.

That's the Jacob I know, she thought, reassured.

As they tired of the rigmarole of the puppeteer's set-up, the onlookers began drifting away.

While Jacob nosed among the equipment still stacked in Napoli's cart, the Italian began tying red ribbons around the sides of his tent. The inquisitor was particularly drawn to the two trunks there, one of which bore a haphazard pattern of holes in its lid.

Only good manners prevented him from inspecting further. There was something… unsettling about the puppeteer, he felt, which he could not place.

Abby, having watched Napoli intently, introduced herself. "My master, Mr Samuel Pepys, saw you perform at Covent Garden, Signor Napoli," she said. "In 1662, I believe. He was most appreciative."

Napoli turned from his task. "Naturally he was! And, *mi tesoro,* you are correct. I performed at Covent Garden in May 1662. That same October, I played before your King." He paused for effect. "A Royal Command Performance!"

"Aye, Mr Pepys attended the same."

That fully diverted the puppeteer's attention. "Your master is acquainted with the King?"

"Well, he's not my…" She stopped, deciding against explaining her working relationship with Pepys. "Aye, Mr Pepys is Clerk of the Acts to His Majesty's navy - they are well acquainted."

Napoli bowed with a flourish, took Abby's hand, and kissed it. "Your King and I, we are bound in mutual admiration. He asked Signor Napoli… nay, he begged him, 'Perform for me once again!' And I relent. I must, for sure. Thus, I shall perform for His Majesty, here on this river, three days from now!"

"On the 30th?"

Napoli bowed. "At ten of the clock that morning. You must attend, I insist it!" Then, beckoning her close, he added in a hoarse, mock-conspiratorial tone, "His Queen is Catholic, you know?"

Abby, taken aback, said nothing.

"You English are all Anglicans," Napoli went on. "The religion of heathens."

With that, he crossed himself and returned to his work. "Will Mr Pepys attend one of Signor Napoli's performances?" he asked.

"I… I don't know. I hope so." Clearing her head of the strange mood that had descended, she added brightly, "We will surely attend - won't we, Jacob?"

Jacob loped across to join her. "I beg your pardon?"

"I told Signor Napoli that we're eager to witness his performance."

Jacob nodded enthusiastically. "Indeed! I have never seen a puppet play."

Having tied his final ribbon, Napoli stood and stretched his back. "Excellent!" he declared, and clapped his hands once again. "Jacob, would you be so kind as to assist me one last time?"

Instinctively, the inquisitor glanced around for any onlookers who might mock him.

Napoli noticed. Holding out his hands, he said, "Forgive me. I am a consummate performer. I cannot help myself - it is in my blood. *La commedia dell'arte!* You were my stooge, Jacob, and I apologise."

When Jacob tentatively nodded, Napoli concluded, "Please. Help me carry my trunk into the tent, since I must away to my lodgings. My journey here was... arduous."

The larger of the two trunks - the one without holes - proved surprisingly light.

"Costumes - and my precious puppets," Napoli explained.

Having installed it and a couple of sacks inside his tent, the puppeteer used chains and padlocks to secure a flap over the window at the front, and the dividing flaps that allowed him entry at the back. The framework itself had already been chained and attached to the ice.

Abby looked perturbed. "Signor Napoli, a thief could cut the canvas with a knife."

Napoli shook his head smugly. "It is the finest, strongest Italian canvas. No Englishman will cut through."

"I fear they could, sir," she persisted. "And I would hate for your puppets to be stolen."

"Mistress…? I know not your name, *mi tesoro*…"

"Abigail. Abigail Harcourt."

"Well then, Mistress Abigail Harcourt, I tell you this. If anybody should steal the great Signor Napoli's Pulcinella, it would be a crime against Art itself!" He paused, pressing a hand to his chest. "*Non*! It would be a crime against God himself!"

"Signor Napoli?"

It was Jacob, pointing to the cart.

"What is it, Jacob?"

"There remains a trunk in your cart."

The puppeteer threw up his hands in exaggerated dismay. Then, as if struck by a sudden revelation, he snapped his fingers. "Indeed, Jacob, you remind me! Bravo!"

Walking to the cart, he opened the lid of the remaining trunk. "Just in case your English fellows slice through my canvas…"

Napoli reached inside and pulled out a length of chain. "*Andiamo! Bruto! Andiamo!*"

Out jumped a thick-set brown dog with white markings and one ear missing. Its head was broad, its drooling mouth set in a snarl.

Spotting Jacob, the malevolent creature leapt for him, barking manically, eyes glazed with violence, only to be held back by the strained chain gripped in the puppeteer's hand.

"Bruto likes you!" Napoli exclaimed. "He can smell you are English!"

Chapter Eleven

Eel Pie

As the afternoon wore on, the lower end of Temple Street crept closer to the south bank.

Hollers, shrieks and cries of joy rang from all directions - tinkers clanging pans to announce their wares, lads chasing footballs and colliding on the treacherous surface, a woman cradling a basket filled with sweet gingerbread.

"Three ha'pperth for a penny!" went her cry.

Elsewhere, spectators gathered around a game of nine pins, cheering players tossing a ball at wooden cylinders - a pastime more typically seen at Moorfields, in the days before fire and ice.

Smoke curled up from the booths and encampments on the fair's fringes, while men on horseback picked their way across the ice, wary of the black patches that signalled thinner ground.

The first of Duke Hobbes's wherries, fitted with runners and drawn by a single horse, was already in operation. Abby and Jacob spotted it making sedate progress, carrying two passengers toward London Bridge, where great blocks of ice had piled up against the bridge's piers, forced there by the unseen current.

Beneath the Southwark bank, a larger vessel with a bare mast was being adapted for the fair, with two broad wheels at the rear and a smaller one at the front.

"Are they to set sail on the ice?" Jacob asked.

Abby could only shrug. "Who knows what curiosities await?"

The Frost Fair was spreading outward, a shimmering city of wonders untold.

As darkness began to fall, Jacob's stomach rumbled and he slumped, hands on knees. Their first day on the frozen Thames had been an exhausting, if exhilarating, one.

They had also encountered a bewildering raft of characters, whom they were keen to discuss over plates of hot food, washed down with a welcome warmed drink.

"Where shall we dine?" he asked.

"Why, here at the fair, surely?"

Wrapping his coat tightly around him, he shivered. "'Tis fearsome cold. I long for the warmth of my local inn."

"Cast a glance about you, Jacob," Abby replied, doing so herself.

All around was perfectly flat, glowing ghostly pale under the light of the moon. Orange fires burned here and there, flashes of colour in the gloom, hunched figures silhouetted in the flames. And in their ears, the now contented thrum of London, returning to life.

"Is it not magical?" she asked.

"Aye," he conceded with a wistful sigh. "I am mighty glad to have you with me, Abby. Without you, I might never have noticed."

"Oh," she said, "you would."

The Horn Tavern Booth, which had stood near the end of Temple Street that morning, was now set some fair way into it. And still the watermen toiled, lofting canvas and binding oars, so rousing was the prospect of a full purse.

By the morrow, the lines of booths would surely be complete.

The passageway that formed Temple Street was no less crowded at night than it had been by day; if anything, there were more bodies. New businesses had sprung up, attracting dawdling onlookers, while the supper crowd prowled.

Holly, ivy and other festive evergreens draped the tents, and lanterns illuminated the pathways. The mingling odours of roasting meats and burning coal filled the air, the smoke hanging low and pungent, as muffled conversations merged into a steady murmur.

Jacob pushed his way toward the Horn's makeshift counter, followed by Abby. The canvas ceiling was low overhead, and copious clouds of pipe smoke had gathered like a morning fog.

There were more women among the guests than was customary - but then this was more of a festive crowd. Most were wrapped up well, in cloaks and coats and hats and hoods. Despite the twin braziers at the rear of the booth, heating pies and jugs, breath condensed as the revellers conversed.

A line of people was waiting to be served by the flustered woman in charge, and Jacob patiently joined its rear. He enjoyed queueing, he found - it gave him time to ponder.

"What can I do for you?"

Jacob had reached the front of the queue without realising it, so lost in thought had he been (wondering whether fish sleep).

Abby was obliged to nudge him.

"I… I beg your pardon?" Jacob stuttered, shaking his head free of idle thoughts.

The innkeeper exhaled impatiently. *"What can I do for you?"* she repeated louder.

"Stir your stumps, sir!" came the catcall from behind.

Jacob was already beginning to wish he had had his way; that they had repaired to the Inn of the Bishop of

Chester, conveniently near his house. It boasted a better sort of guest. "Two mulled wine…" he began.

"Wine's been drunk, only ale," the woman interjected.

Jacob had had his heart set on mulled wine. "Can you not return to your establishment on Fleet Street and fetch more wine?" he asked.

She leaned in close. A mole resembling a sultana nestled in the crease of her nose, and her frown appeared well-practised. "Indeed I could," she replied huskily. "Had it not been burned beyond repair."

Grimacing, Jacob straightened. "Then I shall take two mulled ales."

"And you shall find my gratitude boundless."

He chose to ignore her sarcasm. "What pies have you?"

"Mutton or kidney." She folded her arms.

"No eel?"

Snorting, she called across to a silver-haired fellow in a flat cap, sucking on a pipe. "'Ere, Willy! Caught any eel lately?"

"Only cold ones," the old man quipped.

"Are you a fisherman?" Jacob asked him.

"Aye," Willy replied. "That I am."

"Just the fellow," said Jacob. "I wonder, can you tell me: do fish sleep?"

Behind him, Abby debated chipping through the ice and abandoning herself to the river.

Each clutching a steaming pewter tankard in one hand and a plated pie in the other, the inquisitors jostled their way out of the Horn. They had decided to take their supper on Temple Street, where Jacob would no longer be the subject of such brazen ribaldry.

Jacob was about to take his first bite of what, he had to admit, looked like a most excellent kidney pie, when Abby cried out, "Mr Pepys!"

Following her gaze, he saw a singularly distressed Pepys heading their way through the throng. Their employer was shaking his head, muttering to himself, and so mired in his own concerns that he nearly barged past them.

"Sir!" Jacob caught his arm.

Pepys swivelled abruptly, anxiety writ large across his face.

For a moment, he did not seem to recognise his faithful inquisitor; when he did, he practically fell into Jacob's arms.

"There you are! Oh, thank the Lord!" he exclaimed. His bulging eyes sought out Abby. "And Abigail, too! Perhaps my prayers are answered."

"What is it, sir?" she asked. "What ails you?"

Throwing an arm around each of them, he pulled them into a huddle.

"I dare not speak of it here," he hissed. "I implore you, accompany me outside these tents."

"What is it, sir?" Jacob asked. "What has happened?"

Pepys's gaze darted about. "I fear I have killed a man."

Chapter Twelve

The Mask

Jacob reached for one of the lanterns hanging near the southern end of Temple Street, but Pepys snatched his arm and urged him leave it be.

"We must work by the moon's light alone," he said.

"Sir, what has…?" Abby tried to ask, but Pepys shook his head, finger to his lips, as they made their way through the crowd.

"'Twas an accident," is all he would say, over-wrought.

Emerging from Temple Street, they found a patchy mist settled upon the frozen river.

The derelict Barge House of Southwark loomed on the south bank, its sagging timbers and gaping holes ghostly in moonlit shadows. The exhausted watermen had retired for the night, content that their work was near completion.

Pockets of people lingered on the ice, their figures half-lost in the mist, picked out by the flickering flames of scattered fires.

Jacob whispered urgently, "Pray tell, sir, how did…"

But Pepys shook his head once again and, without a word, set off towards the north bank. Exchanging uneasy glances, the inquisitors followed.

Ordinarily, the Thames gulls would have been squawking, signalling to their kin, but that night the river was silent. The only sound was the muffled thrum of Frost Fair revellers.

Two or three times, Pepys stumbled in his haste to retrace his steps. Jacob scurried forward to help him up, but he waved him aside.

Only when they had covered half the length of Temple Street did he stop. "Here is where it happened. There is the lantern I dropped when I was attacked," he said, pointing towards a small area of shattered glass.

Peering through the mist towards Westminster, Pepys pointed. "There," he said, shuddering.

Out on the ice stood Signor Napoli's tent, lonely and silent. Further towards the north bank, two men laboured by firelight, erecting a wide, round enclosure of upright poles.

Then suddenly, Abby gasped. Clutching Jacob's arm with one hand, she pointed with the other. "Look, Jacob - dead ahead."

"I see it," he said.

Three lengths of timber, each propped horizontally on an A-frame, formed three sides of a square. Close by, a fourth frame had toppled, sheathed in frost.

At the centre of it all, the ice had changed colour - not pale and silvery, but dark. Dark as death itself.

Abby put a hand to her mouth. "What happened here?"

Pepys, shivering, recounted his tale.

That day, he said, he had met with Lord Belasyse at Whitehall to discuss naval affairs, then later dined with Sir Tobias Mortimer at Lincoln's Inn Fields.

Abby scowled. "Tobias Mortimer? The Member of Parliament?"

"Aye," Pepys nodded. "You know him?"

"'Twas on his word that my father was incarcerated, and so met his death. A vile man, entrenched in his Puritan beliefs."

Pepys raised an eyebrow. "I know him but in passing, through my work - and you have my condolences if your words are true..." Seeing her expression harden, he added swiftly, "And I am certain they are. I confess I did find him rather odd."

He went on to explain how, over supper, talk had turned to the Frost Fair. Pepys had mentioned his intention to visit and meet with his inquisitors there, when suddenly, Mortimer had leapt to his feet and ushered him to the door.

"Sir Tobias was most apologetic. He had kept me from my appointed meet, he told me with great concern, and insisted I depart at once. 'Twas dark outside, and he kindly pressed that lantern into my hand." Pepys gestured towards the broken glass. "Had his company been less stultifying, and his supper fare less bland, I might have demurred."

Hurrying down Temple Stairs after dark, he had encountered a bottleneck of folk crowding the northern end of Temple Street, when his progress ground to a halt. A helpful man had approached, suggesting he skirt Temple Street by walking around the back of the booths, and entering at the Southwark end, where the way was clearer.

"Was anybody about?" Jacob asked.

"The mist was thicker at the time," Pepys replied. "'Twas hard to see. No doubt it concealed the blackguard skulking behind me."

As he made his way south, a sound had alerted Pepys. Turning, he found himself confronted by a figure clad in white, his features obscured by a hideous black mask. They grappled briefly before the assailant shoved him hard onto the ice. "As I fell, crying out in terror, my lantern slipped from my grasp, and I slid inexorably. I heard his footsteps behind me - he was following.

"Then, out of the mist, the cordon appeared, and I knew it meant danger. I cried out. As I did so, a man on skates shot before me, then another. I saw their faces, the shock when they spied me."

He let out a juddering sigh. "There was a third skater behind them… I could not stop, and he had no time to swerve. We collided, and he fell through the barrier. The ice… it swallowed him.

"He was gone in an instant. Not a sound. Only his eyes. I saw his eyes." Pepys shuddered. "Then my assailant let out a terrible roar, of anger or anguish. And then… he too was gone, swallowed by the mist like a wraith."

He sank to his knees, pressing his fingertips against his forehead.

"The Dutchmen," Abby murmured.

"And a man clad in white," Jacob added. "Wearing a black mask."

Abby clasped his wrist. "A costume such as Pulcinella wears? Remember Signor Napoli's sign?"

Chapter Thirteen

Black Hole

A bby and Jacob gazed toward Signor Napoli's forlorn tent, shrouded in mist.

"Pulcinella? The performance I attended at Covent Garden?" Pepys exclaimed, his voice carrying out across the ice.

No one heard. The men building the wooden enclosure had begun sawing; everyone else was ensconced on Temple Street, transfixed by its offerings.

"The puppet is garbed in white, with a black mask," Jacob hissed. "Just as you describe your assailant."

Pepys shook his head. "I fought him, Jacob. He was a man, not a puppet."

Abby recounted their meeting with the puppeteer. "As a performer of *commedia dell'arte*, he may well possess a Pulcinella costume."

But Pepys would not have it. The puppet mask he remembered covered only half the face. "The knave who assaulted me wore a full mask." He paused.

"Are you certain, sir?" Jacob asked.

Pepys groaned. "I can be certain of precious little, Jacob."

"Let's at least discover whether Signor Napoli owns such a costume," said Abby. "We may find it in one of the trunks in his tent." With that, she set off.

Jacob grabbed at her coat. "Nay, Abby," he hissed. "Remember Bruto? The beast stands guard."

They looked to Pepys, who seemed fit to weep after his ordeal.

"A devil-dog," said Jacob, "which could tear through a man's throat."

"Is this true?" Pepys asked Abby.

Grimacing, she nodded.

"Then you shall not risk your lives for my sake..."

Jacob opened his mouth to protest, but Pepys hushed him. "There has been enough death here...Oh Lord, forgive me," he murmured, crossing himself.

Abby reached out a hand to comfort him, thought twice, and drew it back. "This evil was not your doing, sir."

Pepys gazed at her. "Aye, Abigail, 'twas indeed but an accident...yet still, I surely sent that poor man to his death."

"Nay, sir. This was no accident. 'Twas murder - but not by your hand."

"Napoli?" Jacob asked.

Abby shrugged. "We must speak with him at first light."

Jacob, looming over the hunched Pepys, gripped his shoulders. "Did you recognise the scoundrel, sir?"

"Was his hair long and black?" Abby added.

Pepys could only shake his head. "It all happened so quickly…" Then suddenly, he started. "Hold! I remember now. Oaf, Pepys! In my panic to find you, I clean forgot…"

Unbuttoning his coat, he fumbled inside. As he did so, a small card fell to the ground.

Jacob plucked it up and held it out for all to see.

1 🔥

London: Printed on the ICE, on
the River of Thames, December 27. 1666.

"What can it mean?" he asked. "And how did…"

"My assailant must have slipped it into my coat as we struggled," Pepys said, reaching into his pocket. "See here, I wrested this from his wrist, ere he toppled me."

He opened his hand to reveal a marble-sized amber bead, threaded onto a thin leather thong.

Abby took it, peering at the smooth stone. Shaking her head, she handed it to Jacob, knowing his eye for detail exceeded hers.

"'Tis too dark," he said, squinting. "I shall examine it further when we are home."

As he turned to her for affirmation, he found Abby staring - not at the bead, but at the black void in the ice.

"Should we?" she asked.

"Must we?" said Pepys.

Abby shuddered, her mind conjuring a face beneath the surface. A bluish-white face, mouth agape, eyes wide in horror, staring up at her through the frozen darkness.

"Nay," Jacob said quietly. "No good will come of it."

Chapter Fourteen

Conference

London had been in turmoil since the fire, its devastation so vast that it reshaped the city's very fabric. Committees assembled to debate how best to clear the wreckage, rebuild, and ensure such a catastrophe could never happen again.

Parish constables and night watchmen, once charged with keeping the streets safe, found they had no streets to patrol. Most, drawn from ordinary householders, had lost their own homes and had greater concerns of their own.

Others seized opportunity. Hackney coachmen, once confined to designated waiting areas, now clustered at the top of Temple Stairs. Much of London was on the ice, heady with drink and soon to seek their beds - a great many in canvas tents beyond the city walls, despite the bitter cold. Where better to find desperate fares?

And Samuel Pepys was surely desperate. His first Thames Frost Fair had been nothing like the revelry and indulgence he had envisioned. How he longed for his home on Seething Lane, and for his wife, Elizabeth – though he dared not share his woes with her. *Best she be kept in the dark*, he reasoned. *For her own good*. It was not the first time he had thought as much.

His inquisitors, he insisted, accompany him.

They had much to discuss.

Elizabeth Pepys was already asleep in her chamber when Mary Blythe greeted the trio at Pepys's door. All were hungry – Abby and Jacob having abandoned their pies – and she was ordered into the kitchen despite the late hour, to come up with something filling. Since the ovens were cold, her choices were limited, though the plentiful Christmastide leftovers would surely help.

Pepys and his inquisitors retired to his study and closed the door.

The fire in the hearth still burned, kept alight for the master's return. Still the space felt cold, the glass in the windows iced over in crazed patterns and the candle flames feeble.

"Oh my," said Pepys, slumping into his chair. "The woes of this night."

Abby and Jacob took seats opposite, across his desk.

"Tell us your tale once again," she said.

While the kitchen maid arranged a late supper of cold beef, bread, marchpane and mulled sack on his desk,

Pepys did just that. The aromatic steam rising from the brew, laced with cinnamon and nutmeg, brought a modicum of cheer to the room.

Yet, unhelpfully, the details remained the same: the costumed assailant, the shove, the Dutchman's doom. Pepys still blamed himself for the unfortunate fellow's death, and was only reluctantly dissuaded.

As a silence descended, Jacob produced the card that had fallen from Pepys's clothing.

1 🔥

London: Printed on the ICE, on
the River of Thames, December 27. 1666.

"The number one beside a flame," he said, scratching his cheek.

"Printed on this very day," Abby added. "Yet I saw no press."

Jacob flicked the card with his thumb. "Those men we passed, struggling with timber beams…"

"Aye," she said. "You're right. A press was built today at the fair, under our very noses. We must find the printer. Who commissioned that card, and why?"

"What if the number one signifies the first victim?" Jacob asked.

Pepys shifted uneasily in his chair. "But who would wish me dead?"

A clock ticked and the fire crackled.

At length, Pepys spoke up. "If I was not the intended victim, then…"

"Aye, sir," said Jacob. "The Dutchman. Yet the chances of propelling you across the ice, in perfect time to send him to his maker…"

Abby sucked in her lower lip. "Are slim, if not perhaps beyond belief. If they were skating in circles, the timing might be made to work." She turned to Pepys. "Did the other two Dutchman not return, once they saw their friend was missing?"

"I did not stay to see. I ducked beneath a tent flap and fled into Temple Street."

"Is Signor Napoli the masked devil clad in white?" Jacob asked. "The Pulcinella upon his sign surely resembles your assailant, sir. The puppeteer must be our man."

Abby looked unconvinced. "It makes no sense, Jacob. A murderer would disguise himself, not parade in his own costume. More likely, somebody's casting suspicion on him."

"Unless 'tis a double-bluff?" said Pepys.

Abby brought up Napoli's connection with the King and his claims of a Royal Command Performance. "Might His Majesty be somehow ensnared in this crime?"

Pepys puffed out his cheeks. "Let us hope not. The King holds the puppeteer in high esteem, that much is certain. Whether he would trouble himself to stand shivering upon the ice to see him perform is another matter. The Italian's vanity is infamous."

Jacob raised a hand. "There is another suspect to consider, sir. Duke Hobbes, Master of the Company of Watermen and…"

"I know of Hobbes!" Pepys snapped. "A loathsome knave I would ne'er deign to trust."

Jaco's jaw tightened. "I beg your pardon, sir. But there was a confrontation at the fair, 'twixt Hobbes and the three men on skates…"

At the fresh mention of the Dutchmen, Pepys snatched off his periwig and lowered his head to his desk.

Jacob pressed on. "The bead you took from the murderer, sir. Let me inspect it again; it may yet hold a clue." He glanced at the flickering candlelight. "Though I fear I may have no better luck."

Pepys looked up, opened the drawer of his desk and produced a magnifying glass, its brass-rimmed lens set into a wooden handle. "Then perhaps you shall with this," he said, at last managing a smile.

Jacob held the bead up to the glow of an oil lamp Pepys had lit for the purpose. Turning it, he inhaled sharply.

"I see something!" he hissed, as the others leaned in. "Tiny letters, engraved here."

A long silence followed as he traced the faint scratches with his fingernail.

"R.F.," he said at length.

Pepys straightened. "R.F.? What can it mean?"

Jacob racked his brain, but the harder he searched, the blanker it felt.

Abby frowned. "A fellowship?"

"Or a man's initials?" Pepys suggested.

Jacob shrugged. "Richard Fuller?"

Pepys shot him a hopeful look. "You met this man today?"

"Nay, sir. I have never heard of him."

Puffing out his cheeks, Pepys sank into his chair.

"We have much work ahead of us," said Abby.

Chapter Fifteen

Aulay's Frost Fair

*M*orag Cussell and her children made it to the gates of London as crisp orange leaves began dropping from the trees. She wasted no time seeking out the Court of Wards, hoping against hope that her husband's talk of a land claim in High Barnet had some basis in fact.

It did not.

When the clerk told her so - that no such claim existed, that no Alexander Cussell appeared among their records - she could have cried. Instead, she laughed. Laughed so hysterically that she was ordered to leave, bewildered children in tow.

Yet even in her exhaustion and grief, there was one glimmer of hope - she still had the silver the robbers had failed to find. And that was all she needed.

Having walked the length of the island, she was not about to lie down.

Her children needed her.

They stopped first in Southwark, where the lodging houses were as dilapidated as they were cheap. Morag found work scrubbing floors at an alehouse, but the pay was pitiful, and the leftover food she was allowed to take home was often rancid.

One evening, as she scrubbed the steps outside, a man paused to watch her. He seemed too well dressed for the area, and bore an air of practised confidence.

"You work hard," he said, introducing himself as John Godfrey.

He ran a laundry business outside Hackney, he told her, employing women to wash for wealthy clients. He could offer a roof over her head, and good pay. "Once my expenses have been deducted," he added.

She took him at his word, and the next day led her children east through Bishopsgate, out towards the suburbs and the unknown.

What have I to lose? *she reasoned.* Any situation is preferable to this.

The journey, though mercifully brief, stirred dire memories of the trek from Scotland. Aulay missed his father terribly, though Ewan's name was never uttered. Whether Morag found the memories too painful, or whether she still raged at his foolishness, the boy was unsure.

Their first glimpse of Hackney was breathtaking. Under a late autumn sun, the village stretched before them, all open fields and scattered cottages, set around a modest parish church.

Rising above them stood grand Tudor mansions with man-icured estates. Among them, they would learn in time, was Sutton House, built in 1535 by Sir Ralph Sadler, Principal Secretary of State to Henry VIII.

Hackney was a place of wealth and refinement, home to the gentry and those who served them. Many of Godfrey's clients lived there, sending their linens to be washed beyond sight of their expensive homes.

The Cussells were not meant for such a world.

They were bound for the marshlands by the River Lea, a mile from the village – far enough distant that their poverty would not disturb the rural idyll. The "roof over her head" proved to be a damp shack, barely fit for rodents, with a lean-to out back where great iron pots steamed and wooden washboards rotted.

The work was relentless, hauling water, boiling, scrubbing, wringing, drying, all for the rich city men with their luxurious sheets. When Godfrey's expenses were deducted, including rent, there was barely a penny left.

Morag had been duped. Having lost the fire to fight, she would make the best of their situation, she decided.

Ailsa helped, fetching buckets and beating cloth, but Aulay hated the place. The reek of the filth, the backbreaking work, the sight of his mother's hands cracked and bleeding. He wanted no part of it.

Instead, he drifted to the local markets, watching how money moved, how words could deceive, and how dice could be made *to dance. On a good day, he earned more swindling than his mother did washing.*

The years passed in a haze of grey, the Cussells clinging to survival as the lad grew restless.

Come the winter of 1634, when Aulay turned twelve, the snow fell like never before. It carpeted the land and froze the river solid.

Godfrey's workers tried breaking through to haul water, but it was miserable, futile work. Instead, he found other ways to wring labour from them – mending clothes, fetching firewood, candle-making – paid in paltry sums that never quite covered his expenses. Indebted, they would work doubly hard once the thaw came.

One morning, with his mother and sister away delivering firewood, Aulay packed his bag with what little he owned. As he did so, he came across the lump of coal the Newcastle dockworker had given him, and it sparked an idea.

He would find work at London's docks.

It had seemed to him an admirable trade. Perhaps one day, he thought, he might stow away on a merchantman and see distant lands, where the sun blazed and men did not con women into servitude.

Asking for directions to the Thames, he expected to find the great river free-flowing, too indomitable to be curbed by mere weather.

Instead, he found a frost fair.

It was like nothing he had ever seen, a carnival on ice, stretching far west into fog. Crowds thronged the frozen river, cavorting and singing, buying and selling, playing games for money…

Playing games for money.

His fingers felt for the fulhams in his pouch, the mercury-loaded dice old Bill Bailey had given him back in Hackney.

A wily old salt, Bill had taken to the lad, felt sorry for him. He had taught him the ways of the cheat, a means to supplement his poor mother's meagre income.

Aulay had learned fast. He mastered slurring, palming and knapping – devious arts of controlling the dice – and soon was fleecing unsuspecting visitors, drawn in by that innocent young face.

Playing games for money, *he thought.*

Aulay dashed onto the ice, and fell flat on his back.

Once among the crowds, he cut a few purses. It was too easy – folk were too rapt by the wonders on offer to notice his delicate fingers slip inside their clothing.

He liked it here, he decided; he felt free, even wished he had absconded sooner.

A short distance away, he spotted a lad dealing out playing cards, his back warmed by a barber's brazier. Men were gathered around, thrusting coins at him.

Ay-ay, thought Aulay, making for the group.

This lad, a few years older, was good – better than him. There were no cards up his oft-darned sleeves, but he did not need them. His hands were quick and his mouth quicker, keeping his crowd amused until the moment he pocketed their wagers.

But he was pushing his luck and one or two were growing restless. One man squinted at the single penny in his hand; others exchanged looks with their neighbour.

"Dice, gents?" Aulay asked, stepping forward. "Game o' Hazard?"

How those guileless men's eyes lit up. A mere child – with dice – easy pickings, they thought. A chance to win back what they had lost.

Except, of course, that is not what happened.

The lad with the cards hovered, watching intently, as Aulay first lost a little – funded by his pickpocketing escapades – then began to win.

He spotted the loaded fulhams, saw Aulay swap them out when one or two men grew suspicious, and recognised the practised hands of a cheat, ever in motion.

The lad was impressed. A smile crept over his face.

"Ho! You there!"

A figure pushed through the crowd, heavy coat flapping, all bluster and authority.

The lad grabbed Aulay's wrist and pulled him away. He had just enough time to scoop up his dice.

They ran laughing, slipping comically on the ice, while their pursuer lost his footing and fell with an audible crack *onto his backside, to the raucous delight of the onlookers.*

At the edge of the fair, breathless and grinning, they stopped.

The lad slapped Aulay on the back. "Not bad!"

It filled the bereft Scottish lad with pride. "Aulay Cussell," he offered.

"Jim Quigley," the lad replied, tilting his head. "You familiar with coney-catching?"

Chapter Sixteen

The Coachman's Tidings

Mr Pepys was courteous enough to allow Jacob to sleep beside him that night, anxious not to disturb his slumbering wife. The shared bodily warmth was a welcome comfort to both men.

Abby returned home – a mercifully brief journey in the perishing cold. She had offered Jacob the use of her floor once again, but he had politely demurred.

In the event, he wished he had accepted. Pepys slept fitfully, tossing this way and that, crying out nonsensical words as if speaking in tongues. Thus, Jacob lay awake despite the toll of the previous day, beset by the chimes of St Olave's and his employer's elbows.

He was woken, the chamber shrouded in darkness, by Pepys's urgent prodding. "Mr Standish! Mr Standish! The Dutchman's death troubles me even in my dreams, it would please me mightily if you and Abigail would investigate the lamentable crime and put my mind at rest."

When Jacob grunted ascent, Pepys promptly turned over and recommenced snoring.

Come breakfast the following morning, the older man's mood had shifted. Perhaps sleep had done him good - Jacob's lack of it certainly had not - for he was more ebullient, even whimsical. More like his usual self.

Wiping egg yolk from his stubbled chin, he gestured at Jacob with his spoon. "Why, pray, was I so unduly troubled yesterday?" he wondered aloud. "I was not to blame for the heinous act. We should confront this Italian puppeteer. If a crime is committed, suspicion is prone to fall on the foreigners in our midst."

"The victim was also foreign, sir," Jacob pointed out. "Dutch."

"I am well aware, Jacob." Pepys took a slug of his small beer and smiled thinly.

A knock sounded at the main door, followed by Abby's voice.

"Sir, last night…" Jacob ventured.

"I bade you investigate the Dutchman's murder."

Jacob nodded. "Do you still wish it?"

"I surely do, Jacob." Pepys heaped another helping of salted cod onto his plate. "But mark me - since the crime is known only to ourselves and to the blackguard who did commit it, I would have you tread with care. Let no careless word rouse idle tongues. I have no desire to find myself entangled in yet another controversy, after those dark days at His Majesty's court."

Abby appeared in the doorway, layered in yesterday's clothes. "Are we to revisit the Frost Fair?" she asked.

Rising, Pepys bade her join them. "I would not miss it for all the silk in Manila!" he said cheerfully.

Their hackney coachman that morning bore ill tidings that quickly quelled Pepys's jovial mood.

Seated astride one of his two horses up front, he called back to his passengers, "Body found at the Frost Fair last night."

The chill in the cab deepened as Pepys and his inquisitors exchanged looks.

"Under the ice, he was, poor soul," the coachman went on. "Starin' up. Like he'd seen a ghost." He paused, awaiting a reaction. None came; only deathly silence. "Word is, he was one of them skaters. Dutch, I'm told."

Abby found her voice. "Is it... Is it known how he died?"

All three waited, breath held, the only sounds the muffled clip-clop of the horses' hooves and the trundling of the coach wheels through snow and slush.

"Not as far as I know. Some folks sayin' 'tis a bad omen. That the fair's cursed."

The simultaneous exhalations of relief filled the cab with billows of white steam.

"There's a hole in the ice, so I'm told," the coachman added. "West of Freezeland Street. That's where 'tis said he went through."

"Freezeland Street?" Jacob piped up.

"Aye. Others call it Temple Street. Prefer Freezeland myself. More mysterious."

"And where was this body discovered?" Jacob asked.

"Down by the Fleet at Bridewell, taken by the current. There's thin ice down there, where the rivers meet."

Abby squeezed Jacob's knee, eyeing him intently. "Is it still there?"

"Not as far as I know. Heard some constable had it, in a tent up by Temple Stairs."

"*Constable?*" Jacob hissed, as Pepys buried his face in his hands.

"Take us to Temple Stairs forthwith!" the inquisitor commanded.

"I already was, if you remember."

Chapter Seventeen

The Drum

From the top of Temple Stairs, where a crowd had already gathered, it was plain how much the Thames Frost Fair had grown. Word had spread, as was the way in the city.

If there was entertainment to be had, Londoners would find it.

Temple Street was now complete, fully traversing the solid river all the way to Southwark. Seizing their opportunity, the watermen had turned their efforts toward earning fares. Boats were out there, several of them, travelling upon the ice.

"I never imagined I would see the day," Pepys said, taking in his first sight of the fair by daylight. "Ingenious."

The smaller wherries, now set upon runners, bore passengers from one bank to the other, some pulled by men with ropes, others drawn by horse. They journeyed upriver toward Westminster and downriver in the direction of the bridge.

The larger boat the inquisitors had seen the day before, now fitted with wheels, was bedecked with flags and banners, its sail lofted. Passengers on deck huddled beneath a canvas canopy, while at the prow, a man beat a drum, warning of their approach. A line of watermen hauled on a rope, propelling the great vessel forward.

The deep beat of the drum - *Doomp… Doomp… Doomp…* - echoed across the fair, and Abby ached to take a ride on the strange, lumbering beast.

The footballers were out again, as were the players of ninepins, now jostling for space among the sea-coal sleds, theatrical troupes, souvenir-sellers, musicians and tipplers.

Looking eastward along the north bank, boys could be seen perched in the trees of Temple Gardens, spectating a great ring of people that had formed an impromptu bull-baiting arena.

Conspicuous by their absence were the Dutch skaters.

"Look," said Jacob, gesturing. "The Italian."

Out there on the ice, the richly garbed figure of Signor Napoli, his long, black hair distinctive, could be made out working at the locks on his Pulcinella booth.

"Aye," said Abby. "And see there." She pointed toward the foot of Temple Stairs, where a tent was pitched that had not been there the previous day.

They each guessed what lay inside: the cold body of the Dutchman.

"Shall we?" Jacob said.

Abby nodded.

Pepys wrapped his cloak around him and tipped his hat-brim down.

Above them, a pale, wintery sun peeked through clouds that hung low, heavy with the threat of further snow.

The three of them stood before the closed flaps of the beige tent, none bold enough to make the first move inside. It was Pepys who broke the deadlock, casting a reproachful glance at his inquisitors before stepping through.

Inside, two men knelt beside a table, deep in prayer. Upon it lay the unmistakable shape of a man, shrouded in a blanket.

Both men looked up, and Abby and Jacob recognised them at once: the brothers, Cornelis and Maarten van Der Haagen. So it was de Vries, the one who had tussled with Duke Hobbes, beneath that shroud.

As Cornelis and Maarten stood, instantly wary, a tension settled over the tent.

The Second Dutch War still raged, the enemy having claimed victory in the Four Days' Battle that June. Both sides had then suffered heavy losses in the subsequent St

James's Day Battle, off the Kentish coast. In short, there was no love lost between the two nations.

"Who are you?" Cornelis, the taller of the two, demanded. "Does the constable know you are here?"

The space was dim, lit only by tallow candles, their acrid scent thick in the air.

"We are…" Jacob began, but Pepys cut him off.

"I am Samuel Pepys, confidante of King Charles. His Majesty did bid me to pass on his condolences. He is greatly saddened to hear of this lamentable death at the fair."

Abby raised an eyebrow. Pepys was no fool. Invoking the King's name established his authority and would make his words hard to refute.

Maarten stepped closer, peering. "Do I know you?"

Pepys edged back. "I sincerely doubt it."

"But I do," the Dutchman persisted. "You were there last night."

Cornelis moved swiftly, grabbing Pepys by the collar. "You collided with Dirk, did you not?" He jabbed a finger in the direction of the body. "You caused his death."

"I did no such thing!" Pepys said, but his voice was quavering and his eyes were wide with fear. "You are mistaken."

Suddenly, the tent flaps swished open, and a gruff voice barked, "What's going on here?"

Pepys and his inquisitors turned to find a squat, broad-shouldered man standing in the entrance, his puffed face flushed from the cold. A cudgel hung at his belt.

"And who, sir, are you?" Pepys asked, regaining some composure.

"I am the constable here, Archibald Frith," the man snapped, taking a pace forward. "State your business."

He resembled more a dockside porter than a man of the law.

The van Der Haagens talked over one another in their desperation to state their case, but it was Pepys to whom the constable deferred. The expense of his attire - velvet, brocade, delicate lace - was evident even to a man of Frith's lowly station. And anyway… the other men were Dutch.

By the time His Majesty's name had been invoked once again, the constable was demanding the brothers' silence with the threat of a beating.

Abby and Jacob said nothing, listening in admiration as their employer took command of the situation. She caught his eye and shot him a wink, as if to say, *That's how 'tis done.*

As the balance of power shifted, Pepys pressed Frith with a few questions, and it became apparent that foul play was not suspected.

Emboldened, Abby asked why the body had remained on the Thames, rather than being taken to the nearest church. It put the constable in the uncomfortable position of explaining how the local church warden had declined to accept it, citing war tensions and the deceased's foreign birth.

Simmering disdain radiated from the Dutchmen, yet they dared not protest.

"There was one small matter," Frith said as their discourse drew to a close. "I found this on the corpse."

The constable handed Pepys a stiff, folded piece of paper.

At once, Cornelis leapt forward and tried to snatch it from him. The constable, swiftly for one so burly, cracked him across the temple with his cudgel, sending him reeling into his brother's arms.

"Stay there!" he barked. "Or I shall clap you in irons."

Both Dutchmen glared as Cornelis clutched his head.

Pepys passed the paper to Jacob, its edges sealed tight with ice.

"Sir, I dare not risk opening it, for fear it will tear. Best we let it thaw." With that, he tucked it inside his clothing.

Abby nodded, signalling they should leave.

The constable turned to Pepys. "These colleagues of yours, sir – who are they?"

"These, Mr Frith," Pepys replied, hooking his hands into the lapels of his cloak, "are my personal inquisitors."

Frith bowed. "Most impressive," he said, though he had little idea of their purpose. "May I enquire… is there a problem?"

Abby smiled sweetly. "Nay, Mr Frith. I assure you, all is as it should be."

Opening the flap of the tent, she cast a final glance at the Dutchmen. Their icy blue eyes burned cold and their jaws were set.

When they were a safe distance from prying ears, Pepys seized Jacob's arm. "Am I safe?"

"I feel sure you are, Mr Pepys," he said, fumbling for the piece of paper. "My concern is more with this. Those Dutchmen were mighty keen to have it."

Abby placed a hand over his. "Aye, Jacob, let it thaw." She gestured toward the Pulcinella Booth, where a crowd had gathered. "We should visit Signor Napoli. I see his puppet play has begun."

Chapter Eighteen

Pulcinella

Signor Napoli's puppet play was well underway by the time Pepys and his inquisitors joined the crowd of spectators. Rich mixed with poor, some well-dressed against the cold, others trembling in patched and torn blankets, huddled among their neighbours. Children's faces shone with glee, eyes fixed on the stage. Few among them had witnessed such riotous nonsense outside of their own, occasionally turbulent lives.

The puppet action unfolded within a framed stage, against a brightly painted backdrop.

Pulcinella, wearing a flowing white robe with draped sleeves, saggy conical hat and black mask - exaggerated, hooked nose and bulging cheeks, somehow both comic and sinister - was under attack.

"Is that the same costume your assailant wore?" Abby asked Pepys.

He could only shake his head, uncertain.

Napoli voiced the characters in English, with his lilting Italian accent. Pulcinella's assailant, dark-haired with apron and headscarf, was his wife, Teresa - who was not happy.

"Pulcinella, you are the laziest man in all Italy!" she declared, wielding a rolling pin with righteous fury. He had stolen her money, she claimed, and would be soundly beaten for it.

Cowering, Pulcinella jabbered in a high-pitched, crazed voice, offering pathetic excuses and begging for mercy.

With every crack of Teresa's rolling pin against his head, the laughter and cheers swelled. The puppets' wooden arms flailed, and glorious chaos reigned.

Napoli himself was largely obscured behind the backdrop, though his hands and face could be glimpsed above the puppets' heads as he operated the strings and observed their movements.

When Pulcinella tripped, Teresa looming over him for the *coup de grâce*, Napoli slipped into a new, pompous, booming voice, rich with his foreign accent. *"What is happening here?"*

At once, Teresa vanished, replaced by a strutting figure wearing a plumed hat and ostentatious moustache. "I am Il Capitano!" Napoli announced, as this new puppet unsheathed its sword.

Puffing out his chest, Il Capitano proclaimed himself the bravest soldier in all the world and launched into a grandiose account of his battle exploits, each more ridiculous than the last.

So enthralled was he by his own magnificence that Pulcinella crept forward and snatched the sword from his grasp. Letting out a strangled yelp, Il Capitano fell backwards and began pleading for his life.

The audience *hooted!*

Jacob, doubled over, tears streaming down his cheeks, had forgotten all about the cold. Pepys, beside him, was making a valiant effort to contain himself, but his shoulders shook with mirth and his cheeks looked fit to burst.

Only Abby, enthralled as she was by the spectacle, found the whole thing a tad… coarse. Her mind was elsewhere, distracted by the troubling investigation that had fallen into their laps. And she was eager to solve it.

As the puppet play drew to a close, an accomplice of the puppeteer's passed through the crowd, jingling a hat laden with coins and calling for payment for such a peerless performance. Most gave willingly: farthings, pennies, groats, shillings, even the occasional crown, dropped from a height with a flourish, to impress those nearby.

The inquisitors and Pepys (who, despite himself, gave a groat) made their way behind the puppet booth. Inside,

Napoli was packing his precious puppets into their cases. The trunk, which Jacob had helped him carry, was still there. Its position suggested he had been standing on it during his performance.

The inquisitors needed access to that trunk. If a man's Pulcinella costume lay folded within, matters would look bleak indeed for the puppeteer.

But how to gain such access? Abby wondered.

"May we see inside your trunk?" Jacob blurted out.

All eyes turned to him – none more intently than Napoli's.

The puppeteer rose, bemusement flickering across his face, indignation in his eyes. Taking a step forward, he jabbed a finger into Jacob's chest. "You," jab, "wish to see," jab, "Signor Napoli's private possessions?"

The two men stood eye to eye, Napoli compelled to stretch to match Jacob's height.

"I do, sir," Jacob replied.

"And who are you?" Napoli demanded.

"I am Jacob Standish…"

"*No!*" The puppeteer stepped back, slumping gratefully to his normal height. "*No, no, no!*" He threw up his hands, flapping them so wildly he began to resemble one of his own puppets. "I know who you are, Jacob Standish, you ass! I mean to say: who are you to ask this of Signor Napoli, the greatest artist in all the world?"

Pepys saw his moment to step in. "Signor Napoli," he said, bowing. "Allow me to introduce myself. I am Samuel Pepys, Clerk of the Acts…"

And so it went on, until the proud Italian was, at last, placated.

Only then did the puppeteer reveal his mystifying and sorrowful tale.

That morning, he said, he had opened his booth to find his faithful hound, Bruto, missing.

"How could this have happened?" he wailed. "If any man had set foot inside this tent, Bruto would have…" Napoli snapped his fingers and thumb together. "He would be dead."

"Was anything stolen?" Abby asked.

"This was my worry!" Napoli exclaimed, launching into a frantic account of how he had checked each of his cases, only to find nothing amiss.

Seizing the chance, she cut in, "Do you own a Pulcinella costume?"

The puppeteer eyed her with amused curiosity. "*Naturalmente, mi tesoro!* I am the most famous performer…"

"Where is it?"

Napoli hesitated. Then, with an exaggerated sigh, he flung open his trunk, lifting silken costumes in a flurry of colour, digging deeper and deeper, growing increasingly erratic. Panic crept over his face as he upended the entire contents onto the ice.

"Aha!" he declared, theatrically retrieving a short silken white gown from the pile, then a black, half-face mask bearing a hooked nose and bulging cheeks.

Abby looked to Pepys, who shook his head.

"They are not the same," he told her.

"Are you certain?" As she spoke, she spotted something among Napoli's costumes: a small white card.

Deftly retrieving it, unnoticed by the others, she turned it over.

2

London: Printed on the ICE, on
the River of Thames, December 27. 1666.

As Napoli glanced towards her, she palmed it from his view.

Jacob, meanwhile, had been inspecting the tent flaps, and was waggling a finger through a small hole in the canvas. "I fear your hound was shot, Signor Napoli," he said.

Napoli stared at Jacob's finger, angrily shaking his head. "Why? Why would somebody shoot my *bellissimo* Bruto? It is not possible." He gestured around the tent. "Where is his body?"

"Carried away?" Jacob suggested.

"No!" snapped the puppeteer. "No man could bear the weight of my Bruto!"

Abby caught his eye. "But two men…?"

Chapter Nineteen

Hobble Joan

Thoughts swirling, Pepys and his inquisitors retraced their steps to the northern entrance of Temple Street. Jacob, more sure-footed on ice than he ever was on mud or stone, strode some way ahead. Abby had adopted a method of short, sliding steps, which seemed to keep her upright.

Pepys, however - who carried himself with a God-given certainty that he ought to remain upright - slid about wildly, arms flailing, and landed on his rump more than once.

"Curse this foul ice!" he raged, picking himself up for the umpteenth time. "I shall be glad when 'tis gone."

"Then there would be no Frost Fair," Abby pointed out, dusting snow off his cloak.

"Hmm," he conceded.

"Is more than one man involved in this perplexing case?" she asked.

It had been some time since she had been able to confer with Pepys on matters of the mind, so pressing had her inquisitor's duties become. How she missed those evenings in his study, when he had allowed her to set down her brushes and browse his library shelves. His collection of books and pamphlets had felt like Heaven to her, opening a world of knowledge she craved but had so rarely been permitted to glimpse.

"Unless 'twas but one man in possession of a sled," Pepys suggested, noticing a child sliding across the ice on just such a device.

Silently, she cursed herself. "We should have looked for tracks."

"The crowds at the puppeteer's booth would have wiped them away."

Quite so, she thought. A grave notion was clouding her mind - that the two cards, Pepys's and now Napoli's, marked them out as victims. If so, her employer had escaped his fate - for the time being, at least.

"Would anybody have reason to wish Signor Napoli dead?" she asked.

Pepys actually laughed. "Would anybody have reason to wish Napoli dead?" he repeated, chuckling. "Why, half of England, and more, I do not doubt. His tongue is fearful loose and he is staunchly Catholic... Why do you ask?"

She felt for the second card, tucked inside her bodice. "No reason, sir," she said.

As they fell silent, the beat of the drum boat entered her ears - *Doomp... Doomp... Doomp...* - and it sounded ominous.

"I can no longer feel my toes," Jacob grumbled when they caught up with him.

"Then we must find you some warmth and sustenance, Jacob," Pepys said, slapping him on the back.

Setting off down the same path the inquisitors had trod the previous morning, when many booths were still being prepared, they now found a thriving avenue of trade. The air was thick with the enticing scents of spices, roasted meats and baking, while the garlands strung overhead lent a festive air, evoking the spirit of Christmastime. Beneath their feet, evergreen twigs had been scattered, crushed underfoot to keep the ice from becoming treacherous.

London's bells had long since chimed the noon hour when they passed the Duke of York's Coffee House. Despite its inflated prices, the place was so popular that guests spilled out onto Temple Street, hunching over their bowls as they supped.

A broadside or two had been tacked to the booth's canvas walls, but this was no 'penny university' like the coffee houses off The Strand. There, the walls were plastered with pamphlets, notices, advertisements and satirical prints, fostering debate and the exchange of news. This coffee house on the ice was little more than a brisk business venture, a means to turn a healthy profit.

And who could blame its beleaguered owner?

"Mr Evelyn!" Pepys cried. "And Mr Baines and Mr Barker. How fare you, gentlemen?"

Evelyn and his companions had found a spot inside the Duke of York's, and Pepys barged his way through the crush of thick coats to join them. Abby and Jacob followed reluctantly.

"Will you take coffee with us, Sam?" Evelyn asked.

"Sir," Abby butted in. "We should visit the printer as a matter of urgency. The card…"

Pepys ignored her. "I shall," he told Evelyn. "How kind of you to offer."

Evelyn, who had not anticipated paying for Pepys's brew, allowed his mouth to fall open just a little. A pregnant silence descended.

A boy appeared, proffering a freshly filled bowl. Pepys took it, only for the lad to extend his other hand. "Thruppence, sir."

"Thruppence!" Pepys's eyes bulged, then glanced across at Evelyn, who was studiously inspecting his thumb. "Why, 'tis…" Catching Baines's stare, he chuckled unconvincingly and began hunting for his purse.

Evelyn addressed Abby. "You wish to visit the printer? I heard tell that one had set up on Temple Street." He handed the boy his empty bowl. "Then I shall accompany you, if I may?"

Turning to Pepys, he bowed. "I shall leave you in the company of my esteemed companions, Sam, confident you will enjoy an engaging and witty discourse."

Baines stiffened, eyes narrowing, while Barker stared into space.

Pepys's expression was a picture.

Glancing from Baines to Barker, he offered weakly, "We did lately spectate the puppet play."

"Pish!" Baines snapped. "Unholy entertainment for heathens and cokesmates. You should stay here, John," he urged Evelyn, glaring pointedly.

"Aye, John, stay," Pepys practically begged, gladly fishing for coins.

"Poor Mr Pepys!" Jacob scoffed, as he and Abby left the gentlemen to their coffee.

"Aren't they joyless?" She shook her head. "If I had half their money…"

Looking around, they found themselves outside the toy-seller's booth. Barely stocked the previous morning, now it glowed with colour, of painted whirligigs and hobby horses, dolls and toy soldiers. Abby was mesmerised.

"Allow me to buy you a gift," Jacob said, stepping inside.

She caught him by the arm. "Nay, Jacob, I require no gift from you! I…"

Pulling away, he made for the vendor, an old man with a thin grey beard, sallow cheeks and a milky right eye. The wizened fellow was demonstrating a spinning top to a child clinging excitedly to its mother, and waved Jacob away impatiently.

When Jacob turned to find Abby, she was standing stock-still, holding a doll.

"I had a doll just like this as a child," she said quietly, lost in the moment. "My father gave it to me."

"Then you shall have it," he said, gently wresting it from her.

It was an ugly thing, he thought, fashioned from painted clay and dressed in a plain brown woollen robe with a tiny linen coif tied at the neck. Its pottery head was grotesquely outsized, with almond-shaped eyes and pursed lips painted a glossy red.

The toy-seller - one Josiah Rowe, according to his signage - abandoned his indecisive customer and sidled up to Jacob. "Her price is one half-guinea," he croaked. "I crafted her myself. Her name is Hobble Joan." Lifting the doll's robe, he noted, "She has but one leg, you see."

Jacob snorted. "Half a guinea for a doll with one leg?"

Rowe's milky eye somehow glinted. "Hand me a whole guinea and I shall gladly replace the other."

"Jacob, I pray you," Abby cut in. "I don't wish…"

But Jacob would hear none of it, and Abby left the booth with Hobble Joan in her hand.

"You're too kind," she said. "On my birthday, of all days."

Chapter Twenty

The Printer

A line of people and a wooden sign outside alerted the inquisitors to the printer's booth up ahead. It read:

W. Wrathbone. Printer
At the sign of The Phoenix

Beside the lettering, a mystical bird was painted rising from flames, wings spread wide.

Opposite was The Lottery Booth, which was drawing a similarly sized crowd, of onlookers and gamblers. Temple Street was so thronged, it felt as if it had ground to a halt.

"A popular man, W. Wrathbone," Jacob said. "Should we wait our turn?"

"Nay, Jacob. We're inquisitors, remember?"

Spurred on, he took the lead, striding past the waiting buyers and into the printing booth. A few called after him irritably, one even tried to pull him back, but he would not be halted in his mission.

Abby, far less imposing, was not so fortunate. The man who had accosted Jacob seized her, while his wife ranted in her ear, "Who d'you think you are, impudent minx? Think yerself better than us? You wait yer turn like everybody else."

Her breath smelled of porridge.

The husband shoved the beleaguered inquisitor. "Aye. To the back of the line with yer."

Others nearby jeered.

Cursing her frailty, Abby had little choice but to comply. *At least*, she thought, *Jacob made it through*.

Inside, the line of people led to a printing press, much like the one Jacob had encountered during their investigation at Rose's Coffee House on The Strand. That freestanding beast of solid wood, as tall as Jacob, had seemed no less unwieldy. Yet that, too, had been dismantled, hauled in pieces, and rebuilt *in situ*. A marvel of engineering.

That such a machine could be transplanted to the frozen river, there to print quaint souvenirs of the Frost Fair, was a novelty too compelling to be missed.

The printer stood at his press bed, applying ink to the type, his back turned to Jacob. He wore a dark doublet and plumed hat, its three swooping feathers in varying shades of orange.

Across the booth was a table cluttered with the tools of his trade: blocks of type, pots of ink, stacked paper, card. A copper brazier smouldered nearby, giving off only the merest hint of warmth.

On the canvas wall behind the restless line of people, Wrathbone had pinned examples of his work. Among them, Jacob spotted a notice advertising souvenir cards printed with a person's name for sixpence each. Beside it was an excerpt from a poem:

To the Print-house go,
Where men the Art of Printing seem to know:
Where, for a Teaster, you may have your name
Printed, hereafter for to shew the same;
And sure, in former ages, ne'er was found
A Press to Print where men so oft were drown'd.

Instinctively, he glanced down at the ice beneath the massive press.

What if it gives way? he wondered, briefly considering standing on tiptoe.

Turning, he sought out Abby, and was puzzled to find no sign of her.

It only steeled his resolve.

"I beg your pardon," Jacob said, tapping the printer on the back.

"Oi, wait yer turn!" came a gruff rebuke from nearby.

Jacob dared not engage. "I am a friend of this man," he heard himself reply.

With a loud tut, the printer swung around to face him.

The lad could not have seen more than twenty summers. Though his skin was smooth, troubled only by patches of reddish stubble, his blue-green eyes were weary, speaking of hard times past. Black, finger-shaped smears of ink lined his cheeks, and he smelled of it too - cloying, almost metallic, so strong that Jacob fancied he could taste it on his tongue.

"You say I know you?" the printer asked, regarding the inquisitor with suspicion.

"Um, aye, Mr Wrath… William… Will… I am Jacob Standish. We…"

The printer turned back to his press.

"Odd's fish! Will you move?" came a fresh heckle from the line.

"Who is that puckfist?" grumbled another.

Seizing Wrathbone forcefully, Jacob swung him back around and thrust the card under his nose. "Did you print this?"

1 🔥

London: Printed on the ICE, on
the River of Thames, December 27. 1666.

The young man lowered his gaze, the brim of his hat obscuring his reaction. When he looked up again, his features were firmly set. "Nay."

Harrumphing, Jacob leaned into the press and picked out one of half a dozen small cards that appeared to have been discarded. Misprints, he reasoned, or early trials.

Compared side by side, the two cards were identical – same size, thickness and typeface – except Wrathbone's bore a man's name, and Jacob's card, merely a number.

The printer, noticing the same, shrugged. "What of it?"

"You are the only printer on the ice, are you not?" Jacob asked.

Wrathbone shrugged again.

"Who commissioned it?"

The young printer gestured toward the increasingly impatient line of people. "My work's popular, Mr Standish, as you can see. Would you remember each and every face?"

"And yet, this card in particular…" Jacob held it up again. "It bears no name, only a number. The number 1. And a flame."

Wrathbone stared at the card, then at Jacob. After a pause, he sighed. "'Twas the first card I printed, once I set up shop - hence the number 1. The flame represents the Phoenix - my mark of trade."

"Somebody cast him out of here!" came a cry.

"Aye! I'm tired of waiting! Cast him out!"

Jacob held his ground. "You recall not who commissioned it?"

Wrathbone snorted. "I told you, I don't. The man gave no name. Now, let return to my work, sir. My buyers grow restless."

As the printer turned, Jacob tugged him back once again. "Describe him to me."

Wrathbone's eyes blazed. "I told you, I remember him not!" Then, sighing petulantly, he added, "A rough-looking cove. Perhaps a waterman."

Before Jacob could press further, a third man shoved his way between them, squaring up to him, stumps of teeth clenched.

There came a loud gasp, followed by a sharp crack of shattering earthenware.

"William?" came the choked, dry voice.

Jacob swivelled, his assailant momentarily forgotten. Abby.

At her feet, the shattered form of Hobble Joan.

Wrathbone's eyes bulged, and he appeared fit to faint. "Abby? Abigail? Can it be? But…"

As he moved toward her, arms outstretched, she could only stare, open-mouthed, appalled.

"Leave me be!" she wailed, face crumpling, and fled.

Chapter Twenty-One

His Printed Word

E ven with the crowds to weave through, Jacob soon caught up with Abby. When he grasped at her shoulder, she stopped, offering no resistance.

They had run south, toward Southwark, and now stood between a man selling sea-coal by the lump at extortionate prices, and a vendor stirring codlins and cream, the air laden with spices.

Abby noticed none of it.

Her sobs were so raw that she paid no heed to Jacob's questions. Eventually, he gave up asking and simply held her close, cushioning the jolting of her shoulders. Whenever a passerby paused to stare, Jacob glared back until they moved on.

It was several long minutes before Abby could regain her composure.

"Shall we find Mr Pepys?" Jacob asked, studying her at arm's length.

He had grown up among three sisters, had witnessed their tribulations and tantrums - though usually fled at the first rumblings. Pepys, with his air of worldly wisdom, would surely know what to say.

"Nay, Jacob," she replied faintly, dragging a sleeve across her dripping nose. Her cheeks were mottled white and crimson, her eyes red-sore and swollen. "I wouldn't wish to disturb him."

He pulled her back into his embrace. "Who was that?" he asked, nestling his chin atop her head, discovering he enjoyed the sensation.

"My brother," she whispered.

Jacob pushed her away, searching her face. "*Your brother?*"

The codlin vendor looked up from his work.

Abby had told Jacob - told everyone - that her three brothers were dead.

Could it be true - was the printer William Wrathbone also William Harcourt?

Twin tears welled in Abby's lower eyelids. As she blinked, they broke free, cascading down her cheeks, to halt, frozen, on her coat. Her lip quivered, and she lowered her gaze.

Fie, he thought. *'Tis true indeed.*

"What did he tell you?" she asked softly.

Jacob clasped his jaw. "As I began the chase, he called after you…"

She looked up.

"He said he believed you were dead."

They walked on, past bedecked booths promising treats that enticed neither of them.

Emerging at the southern end of Temple Street, they found casks piled haphazardly beside the steps up to Barge House, away from the crowds, and sat.

There, Abby explained everything.

She had lied to Jacob. Lied to Mr Pepys. William Harcourt, eleven months her junior, had survived his brothers, Henry and John. Their father, Ambrose, had apprenticed William at his printing shop while she was sent to Greenwich, to live with Edward Yaxley, her mother's cousin. She had merely dabbled in the family trade, she admitted.

When Yaxley died, she returned to London, only to discover her father gone - incarcerated in the Clink, awaiting trial.

Abby sighed, shuddering at the memory. "As I told you in Brampton, my father was accused of seditious libel, on the word of the Witch-finder General and his associate, Tobias Mortimer. *Sir* Tobias Mortimer," she spat out the word. "They claimed my father had distributed leaflets critical of the witch trial at Essex Assizes, threatening the very order of the kingdom."

Jacob placed a hand on her knee. "And you discovered this...?"

"From William. He alone greeted me when I returned home. He swore to me that he had beaten his fists against the chests of the soldiers who came to arrest our father. That he had defended his piety until his throat grew dry."

"He had not?"

"I found pamphlets in the shop, penned by the same men who had my father arrested. The words of one..." She took a deep breath. "The words of one, I shall remember till my dying day." And she recited:

"The Devil's servants wear many faces, yet all take up the same tool - the quill, the press, the printed lie. In these times, when godly men must stand fast against corruption, we find among us those who would pervert the Gospel under the guise of free thought. Such a man is Ambrose Harcourt..."

"The printer's name was there for all to see," she went on, eyes glazed. "'Neath those same words."

"William Harcourt?"

She nodded. "He pleaded his innocence, fell to his knees before me, told me he'd been offered no choice, lest he follow our father to jail and ruin."

"Did he speak the truth?"

Her expression hardened. "I know not, and care still less. I left, vowing I'd never speak with him again."

Chapter Twenty-Two

The One Stone

With a half-hearted smile, Abby slid off the wooden cask. "Shall we join Mr Pepys?"

"Aye," Jacob replied, standing and stretching. "Where will we find him?"

"'Tis dinner time," she said. "He'll be filling his stomach."

Unwilling to face the rows of booths, the prospect of encountering her brother too painful to contemplate, Abby led them instead toward the enclosed Ox Roast out on the ice. They had seen it being built on the first night of the fair, and now smoke and the aromas of roasting drifted eastward, carried on the wind toward the tightly packed crowds on Temple Street.

Pepys had eyed it greedily when they arrived that morning, and had suggested they dine there later. He was, they agreed, a man of his word.

"I found a second card among Napoli's costumes," Abby said as they walked. "Identical to Mr Pepys's, but bearing the number two."

"Why did you not tell me?"

"We were with Signor Napoli at the time, and I didn't wish to alarm him. What if my deductions are awry?"

"What are your deductions? I confess, I find myself in the dark."

"That the puppeteer will become the second victim. If Mr…" She trailed off.

The frozen river, as far as the eye could see, teemed with people – eating, drinking, slipping, sliding, selling, buying, praying, playing, dancing and singing – but one had caught her eye.

Some twenty yards ahead, a man stood in a hooded vermillion robe, wearing a black, full-face mask. Around his neck was hung a wooden placard that read:

DEATH Stalks this HEATHEN Fair
BEGONE or Face HIS Wrath

Abby nudged Jacob, pointing. "The mask," she said.

At once, he set off toward the figure, Abby hot on his heels.

When they reached him, only a single curling lock of black hair, spilling from behind that leather mask, offered any clue to his identity. The eyeholes were set deep, such that he appeared unseeing, and the expression on the mask was utterly blank.

Both Abby and Jacob felt his chill.

Slowly, deliberately, he turned and began walking away.

"Stop him, Jacob," she hissed through clenched teeth.

Jacob lunged forward and seized his arm. They struggled, until the hooded man wrenched himself free and broke into a trot.

At that moment, a football shot past Jacob's feet, followed by the lad pursuing it. The two collided, crashing to the ice.

Ahead, the vermillion robe was swallowed up by the milling crowd.

"Did you…?" Abby began, helping him to his feet.

"Feel I knew him?" he interjected. "Aye," he said. "And more - I swear a felt a bead at his wrist as we grappled."

"Marble-sized, like that Mr Pepys snatched from his assailant?"

He nodded.

"If you're right, Jacob, then 'R.F.' is not one man… but an organisation."

Mr Pepys was indeed at the Ox Roast. Evelyn and his companions, they noted with relief, were nowhere in sight.

"Abigail! Jacob!" he called out on seeing them. "Come, join me! This ox is exquisite!"

Behind him, an entire beast, browned and charred, hung suspended over a crackling wood fire. Sheltered within the enclosure, diners stood crowded around it for warmth, steam rising from their food as they picked at it with burning fingers.

When they were furnished with meals of their own, wrapped in bread and dripping with thick gravy, Jacob began the tale of Abby's long-lost brother.

She implored him not to trouble their employer with her personal woes, but Pepys cut her off. "I would hear the story," he told her.

When Jacob had finished, Pepys turned to Abby. "What if your brother spoke the truth? That refusing to print the pamphlet denouncing your father would have led to his execution?"

Angrily, she tossed her half-eaten meal into the fire. She dared not open her mouth, lest a torrent of pent-up emotions spew forth.

"His words ring true, Abigail," Pepys persisted. "Men have perished for lesser reasons."

"He seemed to me bright and industrious," Jacob added.

These men, she thought contemptuously, *defending their ilk*. "That printing press was my father's," she said. "William stole it from him."

"Did he not take it on after your father's arrest, having been apprenticed by Ambrose himself?" Pepys asked, looking to Jacob for assent. "I understand your feelings, truly I do. My own brothers have caused me considerable distress with their indiscreet and wanton ways. I would counsel…"

Abby could bear it no longer. "What would you have me do?" she snapped.

Pepys took a step back; never had he seen her more ferocious. "I do beg your pardon, I… I would not wish to interfere, however…"

Yet you have *interfered*, she thought, then caught herself… His intentions were kind-hearted. She saw the same concern in Jacob's eyes.

Rubbing her cheeks, she sighed. Her face felt hot. "I cannot forgive him."

Pepys took her hand. "But perhaps you could allow William to explain his actions?"

I already did, years ago.

But Pepys was not done. "I wish to place a wager at The Lottery Booth," he said. Then, smirking to himself, added, "Perhaps, since your brother's printing booth is close by, we might *kill two birds with one stone?*"

When she showed no glimmer of recognition, he was obliged to explain that Thomas Hobbes had coined the phrase in his 1656 work, *The Questions Concerning Liberty, Necessity, and Chance*, "Which seems rather apt," he concluded, only to be met by the same blank stare. "Your brother acted through necessity, you see, whilst I shall rely on chance!"

Abby could not force a smile.

She imagined that one stone in the palm of her hand, feeling its weight, its curves and sharp corners - then hurling it with all her might.

Chapter Twenty-Three

Bleak Alley

Abby's steps grew leaden as they neared the bottle-neck of folk gathered at the printing and lottery booths. Hours had passed since their last visit, yet the popularity of neither had waned – if anything, the crowds had only increased in size.

Sensing her reluctance, Pepys chivvied her along. "Come along, Abigail – there is nought to fear!"

But there was, she knew, all too well.

Ambrose Harcourt's wife, Mary, gave birth to a son and a daughter within the space of a year, their youngest, Henry, having succumbed to consumption in infancy.

It had not been planned that way – Ambrose's printing business in Southwark provided little more than a subsistence living – but fate had decided otherwise. The narrow passage on which they lived was named Beak Alley, though the locals, with typically English humour, knew it as Bleak Alley.

The Harcourts' was a run-down, crooked house, more than a hundred years old, once belonging to Ambrose's father, and his father before him. The plaster crumbled, the beams split, and the old thatched roof resembled a briar patch, yet it held together, as determined as its inhabitants.

Ambrose ran his printing workshop on the ground floor. The moment he turned his back, the children would swarm over the lumpen press, racing to claim its summit. Its smell lodged in their clothing and hair, the black of the ink on their hands and faces. Their father would pluck them off, one in each fist, warning of the dangers of the great machine.

It never stopped them, since they were unstoppable. A blur of wide-eyed anticipation.

Brother and sister were rarely apart. He followed her everywhere, worshipped her, a shadow in grubby breeches. Southwark's stinking streets became their kingdom, where an old barrel was a castle and stray hounds, invading armies.

They hunted for gold in the guttering drains and stole apples from nearby orchards. If one were caught red-handed, dragged home by the collar, the other would protest their mutual innocence until both were boxed about the ears. Punishment shared felt like punishment halved.

Mary Harcourt grew adept at stretching a pan of vegetable broth over three nights and making a loaf last a week. She cooked downstairs, hemmed into the only space not already taken up by her husband's piled pamphlets, type-cases, quoins, galleys, ink-rollers and mallets.

The family slept upstairs in the loft space, among straw and weevils.

It was a harsh but rewarding existence, each new dawn feeling suitably well-earned.

Then, one bitterly cold night in February 1656, everything changed.

Mary was with child once again - a brother or sister for Abby, then ten, and Will, nine. But the birth did not go to plan. The midwife failed to appear, and though neighbours rushed to Mary's bedside, alerted by her agonised cries, neither mother nor child - a boy, named John - survived the ordeal.

Though such tragedy was commonplace, it struck Ambrose hard.

For weeks, he sought solace in the alehouse, abandoning his children to their own devices - where, despite everything, they thrived in their own unruly way.

Only when Will accidentally set fire to a stack of rejected proofs, and once again the neighbours came to their aid, did Ambrose rouse from his self-pitying stupor.

After that, he toiled twice as hard, allowing the children as much responsibility as he dared.

Abby would later realise it had been the making of her.

As brother and sister grew, Ambrose granted them greater responsibility: setting and inking the type, collating and folding the printed pages. Abby, he noticed, took to the task with more spirit and thought than her brother, which was awkward, since Will was the natural heir to the business.

But he loved them equally, so indulged them both.

When the printing tasks failed to sate her enquiring mind, he set about teaching her to read and write. It was not the done thing, which appealed to him.

Ambrose Harcourt was an honest man and a devout church-goer, self-educated through the very publications he printed. He could quote Cicero, expound upon the latest astronomical theories, and debate - with surprising enthusiasm, given he had tasted neither - whether coffee or chocolate was the superior drink.

There was but one aspect of his life he would never share with his family. Through his printing connections, he had fallen in with a circle of radical thinkers - men who railed against tyranny, state-imposed religion, and the creeping tide of superstition.

It was at their urging that he printed pamphlets critical of those in power, advocating reason over hysteria, peace over aggression.

By then, Abby was in Greenwich, sent to live with her mother's cousin, Edward Yaxley. The air was cleaner there, and Ambrose knew the Yaxleys owned a fine library that his daughter would devour. It meant one less pair of hands, but equally one less mouth to feed. Fortuitously, given the sheer number of hours he had worked at it, Will had become a useful, even willing, printer's apprentice.

Ambrose printed his most controversial tracts after dark, when his son was safely sleeping. He had built a network of distributors - furtive men who came out at night - whom he trusted with his life.

It served him well, until the night one such man fell foul of the law. Accosted by a watchman on the night-time streets of Westminster, his bag was searched and pamphlets discovered, denouncing the 1645 witch trials at the Essex assizes.

Ambrose had omitted to append his name to them. But a man's tongue is easily loosened by the turn of a thumbscrew.

One golden dawn, a pounding came at the door of the Harcourt home on Beak Alley. All around, shutters inched open and ears strained as men in uniform burst in, hauled Ambrose from his bed and dragged him to a waiting cart.

William, then 15, lay still as the dead in his bed, not daring to make a sound. When footsteps thundered up the stairs, he leapt out and hid under sacking.

Abby knew nothing of this, secreted away in the suburbs, head buried in a dusty tome.

Only after Edward Yaxley died, and she became a burden on his family, did she return to Southwark. There, she discovered her beloved father had died in jail while awaiting trial, and her brother operating his press.

The siblings wept as they embraced, overjoyed to be reunited, yet bound in grief. Everything Will told her, she believed. Why would she not, when their loyalty was sacrosanct?

And so, orphaned Abby found herself back in Beak Alley, the plaster more crumbled, the beams further split, dwelling among the ghosts of the past.

Helping Will at the press, they took on more work. Business was, if not brisk, at least sufficient to put food in their mouths. Despite the undercurrent of sorrow, they rediscovered their bond, recounting childhood escapades, relishing each other's company.

Yet as the weeks passed, Abby grew wary of certain men who frequented the shop - men with dour expressions, who quoted Scripture and eyed her with undisguised contempt. When she confronted Will about them, he grew flustered and evasive.

After they left, he would work late into the night, forcing her back upstairs if she went to investigate.

Come morning, when no freshly printed pamphlets were to be found, he would tell her they had already been collected.

It was his secrecy that drove her, one morning while he was at the market, to turn the place upside-down.

And there, in a corner of the eaves, buried beneath musty old blankets, she found it.

Among a pile of discarded printings lay the pamphlet condemning their father.

Printed by his son.

The one bearing those words she could not forget.

She left that day without a word, and never looked back.

Chapter Twenty-Four

Childermas

Jacob could see it in her face; those bright turquoise eyes seemed empty. When he took her hand and squeezed it, her face remained blank.

Pepys pushed his way through the throng, heading for the Wheel of Fortune.

It struck Abby that he hated parting with his money, and that his sudden urge to gamble might be less about chance and more a ploy to draw her into her brother's orbit.

Gaze inexorably drawn, she took in her his sign.

W. Wrathbone. Printer
At the sign of The Phoenix

Wrathbone? she thought. *How dare he disown us?*

Inside the Lottery Booth, barely controlled chaos reigned. Men jostled and shouted, barging past one another to place bets on the brightly coloured spinning wheel.

Divided into twenty numbered sections, it alternated red, yellow and blue, each segment separated by a wooden peg set at the rim.

At the top, a metal pointer clacked against each passing peg, its rhythm slowing as the wheel lost momentum. At first, the colours blurred into one, until gradually they came into focus, while the men's cries rose in anticipation, urging their chosen numbers on.

One man, dressed as garishly as his wheel, commanded the space. Heavy-set and booming, he wore a riot of mismatched fabrics, and his doublet fitted so tightly, it seemed as though his head might burst.

This was Septimus Sprig, according to his sign.

"Pay a penny, win a crown!" Sprig cried. "Step up, gents! Fortune favours the bold!"

Jacob stooped to whisper in Abby's ear, "His wheel is a tad off-centre. It will favour certain numbers over others."

Ordinarily, she would have relished his insight. But behind her, not 20 yards away at his press, was her brother, and she could sense his presence.

Could he sense hers?

"Outta my way!"

Abby's reverie was shattered as two men broke through the throng.

"Septimus Sprig!" one growled. "You owe me money."

Incredibly, the booth fell silent. Only the *clack-clack-clack* of the pointer on the pegs could be heard as the wheel slowed. All eyes watched as it teetered to a halt at the number 13, followed by a chorus of groans. Nobody had bet on 13.

"He's a cheat!" came the cry, to a rumble of assent.

"Indeed, sir! For he cheats the watermen of their livelihoods!" Duke Hobbes declared, planting his peg-leg on the frozen ground.

Behind him was the man the inquisitors knew as Carter - a feisty, ferret-faced cove with broad shoulders and raw, scarred hands, perhaps once burnt.

"This booth is unlicensed!" cried Hobbes.

Catcalls rang out, alongside the odd, "Hang him!"

But Sprig was not easily intimidated. When the dishevelled old man who recorded the wagers sidled in beside him, he elbowed him away. "I need no licence, Duke Hobbes. My booth is sanctioned by His Majesty the King, to raise monies for the royal purse."

"No wonder he's so rich!" some jester called out.

Few laughed, conscious of their own empty purses.

Hobbes pushed his face into Sprig's. "These stout booths were erected by the Company of Watermen and Lightermen for the purposes of licensing. Now, pray, where is your licence?"

Sprig's spaniel-eyes fixed mockingly on his accuser, and he rolled up his sleeves, prepared for fisticuffs. "Are your ears stuffed with snow, waterman? I told you, I need no licence." He paused, enjoying the expectant hush. "Or will you take up your grudge with the King?"

Growling like a cornered animal, Hobbes turned on his heel. Shoving Carter, who stumbled into the man behind him, he spat out his parting words. "I shall return."

For a moment, silence hung in the air. Then, as if nothing had happened, The Lottery Booth returned to life, a heaving mass of desperation and loss.

"I think I shall save my pennies for another day," Pepys said, patting the purse beneath his cloak. "By the by, did you notice the legend on the wheel?"

Jacob glanced up. "Rota Fortunae?"

"Aye," Pepys replied, "'Tis the Latin for 'Wheel of Fortune'. And it occurred to me…"

But the light had already dawned in Jacob's eyes. "R. F.," he said. "Is Sprig involved in the Dutchman's death?"

The inquisitor's neighbour, his arm trapped behind Jacob's back in the crush, butted in, "That foreigner who fell through the ice? I heard he stole money from Sprig's booth."

The man behind him joined in. "I 'eard 'e was a Spanish spy!"

Then another. "He weren't Spanish, he was French!"

Pepys looked up at Jacob pleadingly. "May we leave this awful place?"

As Abby forced her way past a woman carrying a swaddled baby, there he was: her brother. William.

Taller than she remembered, but those eyes, so often remarked upon, so like hers. And he was smiling. Beaming, even.

Before she could react, he had enveloped her in his arms. "Oh, Abby! How I've missed you."

Forcing her hands between them, she pushed him away. "Leave me be!"

On either side, Pepys and Jacob stood frozen and voiceless.

William's smile faltered, replaced by something more pleading. "Let me explain."

Her fists clenched and unclenched. "I told you three years ago - our words are done."

Pepys stepped between them, hands raised. "Perhaps I might… act as moderator?"

Abby shook her head furiously, eyes to the heavens. "Can nobody hear me?"

Rounding Pepys, William reached out for her hand. She recoiled.

Shocked, he stepped back. "Perhaps, if this kind gentleman might be allowed to…"

But Abby's eyes were blazing. "What day is it today, William?"

Flustered, he rubbed his cheek, leaving a dark smear. "Why, 'tis the 28th day of December. Anglicans know it as Childermas. Feast of the Holy Innocents."

Her lips curled into a smirk. "*We are Anglicans*, yet you seem to forget. Admit it, I mean nought to you."

She gave him no chance to respond. Turning sharply, she was gone.

"'Tis her birthday," Jacob whispered, passing William in her wake.

"Jacob!" Pepys called after him. "Await me at The Horn Tavern Booth."

Chapter Twenty-Five

Aulay & the Coney

*J*im Quigley took Aulay Cussell under his wing, deep in Whitechapel's underbelly.

He taught him how to speak like a Londoner, since his Scottish accent made him stand out like a cross on a plague door, and gave him a cap to cover his bright orange hair.

He tutored him in the art of coney-catching: deceiving a mark by any means necessary, to take them for all they had.

He taught him nipping, foisting and cross-biting. He even explained the practice of prigging, though he had never tried it himself, he confessed, being unable to ride a stolen horse.

They shared a room in a crumbling tenement on the broad road that led out toward Essex. Each floor was a maze of dark, doorless rooms, whose inhabitants would vanish like fleeing rats at the first cry of authority. The place was thick with the stench of tanneries and the salt air drifting up from the docks.

Whitechapel never slept. Carts clattered past, hauling fish, coal and tallow. Sailors brawled in the taverns, women bel-

lowed from high windows, and hawkers hollered their wares, pushing rotten fruit and spoiled fish onto whichever swill-belly would take it.

Aulay loved the place.

The conditions may have been no better than those his mother had endured, but the life there... it burned brightly.

And the Quigley-Cussell partnership thrived.

There were near scrapes, when a night watchman caught them breaking into a warehouse, or they were chased by sailors fleeced of their grog money. But they were familiar with the narrow backstreets, knew enough of the locals to be shepherded through a doorway when a constable gave chase.

Agile and wily, they dodged the ever-present hand of justice. Neither grew rich; in truth, their bellies often rumbled, but their hearts and minds were sated.

Then, one day, they encountered Thomas Langridge, and everything changed.

It went like this:

The name Tommy Langridge carried weight around the dockyards. He owned taverns and gaming dens, command-ed a network of dubious associates, and boasted friends in high places. Word was, he was expanding his operation into Whitechapel.

He was also a corrupt money scrivener, lending at exorbitant rates and twisting contracts so that debts never disappeared.

It explained why Margery Bell, who ran her late husband's haberdasher's shop, found herself dragged into the street one morning, scratching and screaming.

Her shop sat opposite Aulay and Jim's tenement, and the commotion drew them outside.

Two thick-set brutes with flat noses and bulldog chins had pushed Margery to her knees. A third man, wearing a tall, feathered hat and jaunty cape, stood imperiously over her.

"But my debt is paid, sir!" she pleaded.

"I assure you 'tis not, Mistress Bell," the caped man replied. "You sleep above your shop, do you not?"

She nodded, yet plainly baffled.

"Then where is my rent?"

"But... but I own the shop, sir. 'Twas my late husband's. He..."

"And you signed it over to me, in lieu of our arrangement." He thrust a sheet of parchment in her face. "Here - is that not your mark?"

Struggling, trapped in the grip of the stooges, she howled indignantly. "You tricked me!"

Langridge rolled up the parchment with a smile. "Come now, Mistress Bell. We have a contract, and you must honour it."

One of the henchmen shoved her into the mud.

She rose, clasping at her face in desperation, streaking her pale cheeks with filth. "I beg you, sir, take my lace!"

Langridge let out a hollow laugh. "What need have I of lace? 'Tis coin I deal in."

Aulay's teeth clenched. He had seen enough and moved forward, but Jim pulled him back.

"That's Tommy Langridge," Quigley hissed.

Langridge turned, meeting Aulay's stare.

"Ransack her shop," he ordered his men, tipped his hat with a wink at Aulay, and turned on his heel.

Blows were almost traded over Aulay's determination to seek revenge on Margery Bell's behalf.

"She'll neither know nor care," Quigley pointed out.

But Aulay would not be swayed, and Quigley's loyalty would seal his fate.

They disguised themselves as merchants, in slashed doublets and silk breeches, stolen to order, and wide-brimmed felt hats. But their features were haggard, their demeanours born of poverty, which no amount of expensive fabric could conceal.

Claiming to be Scottish wool traders, they sought out Langridge at The Black Swan, a dockside tavern he was known to frequent.

Joining a rowdy group of dockworkers, Aulay ordered drinks for the table, his natural accent thick with sack as he boasted of a deal that would make them all rich.

"I've a warehouse full o' the finest broadcloth," Aulay declared. "Ye'll triple, nay, quadruple yer money." Then he leaned in, lowering his voice, as if letting them in on a secret. "Straight *fae the looms o' Scotland, it was, meant for the court itself - till the buyer broke contract. Now it sits, gathering dust, waiting for the right man to take it off ma hands."*

Tipping back his drink, he grinned. "If yer money's good, lads, I'll make ye rich."

The scraping of stool legs signalled Langridge's rise.

The dockworkers fell silent, returned to their ales.

"I may be interested in your scheme," Langridge said.

Aulay's jaw tightened. "Oh aye?"

Jim Quigley tried his best to look imposing.

"Aye," Langridge mimicked.

Aulay licked his lips. "Well, then… my deal is open to all, sir."

Splaying his hands on the table, Langridge leaned in. "Do I know you lads?"

They could only shake their heads, mute with contained fear.

"And d'you know me?"

Aulay snapped, faced him off. "Aye. I know you."

Langridge locked his fingers around Aulay's wrist. "Then you'll know I can spot a half-baked con from a mile away."

His two henchmen appeared behind him, arms folded, scowling.

With a flick, Langridge sent Aulay's hat tumbling to the floor, revealing his shock of orange hair. "The only true part of your tawdry tale is you're a Scotsman." He snorted. "Seize them."

Jim Quigley was away before Langridge's command had even left his mouth.

Aulay was not so fortunate.

Chapter Twenty-Six

Debs Corbet

Jacob was still consoling Abby when Pepys found them sheltering inside the tavern tent a few minutes later. Her eyes were bloodshot, and there were no drinks in their hands.

From out on the river came the unmistakable rhythm of the drum boat.

Doomp… Doomp… Doomp…

"Mr Pepys!" the lady innkeeper cooed when she spotted him. "Yoo-hoo!"

Pulling down his hat brim, he turned his back on her and fumbled for his purse. "That awful woman. Her voice can be heard in Islington," he muttered, handing over a crown. "Fetch mulled wine for us, Jacob."

"I… I don't want…" Abby began to protest.

But Pepys would hear none of it. "Nonsense," he said. "The warmth will do you good."

"Sammy Pepys, as I live and breathe!"

Not to be outdone, the innkeeper had joined him.

"Were that you did not," Pepys muttered under his breath. Then, turning, he offered her a forced smile. "Mistress Corbet, such a pleasure to make your acquaintance, however I am conducting private business..." he motioned at Abby.

"Ohhhh!" she cut in, winking theatrically. "I see! Well, I would never wish intrude upon a gentleman's *private business*, would I, sir? Last time I saw you, you were conducting *private business* with that other..."

"*Mistress* Corbet," Pepys said, eyes darting about the tent, ushering her back towards her counter, "my good friend, Mr Standish, awaits your service. He is eager to sample your mulled wine," he raised his voice, "*are you not, Jacob?*"

Jacob, obligingly, waved, as Debs Corbett curtsied extravagantly and bustled back to her counter, twittering gaily to herself.

Pepys, mortified, surveyed the assembled drinkers. A departing couple moved aside, revealing three men who had been previously obscured from view - Evelyn, Barker and Baines, nursing small ales, the two younger men glaring in appalled silence.

Pepys found a spot outside the tent, among so many others engrossed in their own discourse.

"Abigail," he said, in a tone he hoped sounded fatherly. "I have spoken with your brother, and he has given me his side of the story. Would you hear it?"

Before she could reply, he pressed on. "Soldiers came for your father, Ambrose, when William was working with him as an apprentice. He fought with them as best a boy could, and they arrested him. Were you aware of that?"

Though Abby was in no mood for an inquisition, she owed Mr Pepys respect - indeed, a great deal more. So she bit her tongue. "That's what he told me, sir." Still there was an edge to her voice she could not disguise. "Yet it cannot excuse..."

Pepys raised a hand for silence. "Pray, hear me out."

Jacob, looming over them, supped nervously.

According to William, the soldiers ransacked the printing workshop on Beak Alley that morning, seeking further evidence. But Ambrose had been prepared for such a day, secreting his seditious materials beneath the floorboards in the loft, where they remained undiscovered.

Still, the authorities had the pamphlet - the one condemning the witch trials and the zealous men who hunted the poor women down. They also had the distributor's word that Ambrose was its printer.

Abby's father was taken to Newgate Prison for interrogation, while William was given a choice: testify against him or face the same charges as an accomplice.

The severity of the offence was impressed upon him, and he crumpled.

Without the press, he had nothing. He would have been cast into the streets to live out a brief and desolate existence.

So he cut a deal with Sir Tobias Mortimer and the Witch-finder General. They would not confiscate the workshop - provided he began printing tracts in favour of their cause.

"He was fifteen years old," Pepys told Abby. "What would you have done?"

She brushed a long strand of hair from her face. "I would have died at my father's side."

Pressing his palms together, Pepys held them to his nose-tip and smiled. "We are not all cut from the same cloth, Abigail."

"I'm hungry," she said.

As they were eating, a strange event occurred.

While discussing their return to the fair on the morrow, a lad, no more than ten years old, approached Pepys. Tugging at the back of his cloak, the boy was met with a dismissive wave, but proved insistent.

With his back to the inquisitors, Pepys bent down and the lad spoke to him covertly.

When he straightened, he appeared out of sorts.

"What is it, sir?" Jacob asked. "What did he say?"

"A message from the Navy Office, of some urgency," Pepys replied distractedly. "I shall be unable to accompany you to the fair tomorrow."

Though neither inquisitor entirely believed him, it was not their place to question.

They did, at least, finally manage to finish one of Debs Corbet's kidney pies - and it was, indeed, delicious.

Wary of passing the printing booth, the three made their way toward Southwark. Approaching the end of Temple Street, they were hit by an icy gust of wind.

Up ahead, one of the booths had collapsed, its poles lying skew and its canvas gathering snow. Beneath it was huddled a woman with a bundle clutched to her chest. Two small children, a boy and a girl, clung to her sides, shivering in the dusk.

From the opposite direction came the familiar figures of Hobbes and Carter.

At the broken tent, Hobbes stopped to inspect the damage.

Carter, meanwhile, seized the little girl by the scruff of the neck and tossed her aside, while her mother cried out, trying to shield the boy.

The weaselly waterman only sneered. "Outta the way, you lice-bitten rats."

Pressing a coin into the woman's hand, Hobbes confronted him. "Leave her be," he growled.

Carter took a step back, muttering something under his breath, as Pepys and the inquisitors passed.

Hobbes paid them no heed.

Chapter Twenty-Seven

Deductions

Abby and Jacob set off on foot toward his house on Strand Lane. Pepys bade them good night and took a coach to Seething Lane.

It had been another exhausting day, filled with revelation and death - quite enough upheaval for any inquisitor.

The church bells were tolling the tenth hour when Jacob ushered Abby into his parlour. They sank heavily into fireside armchairs, still clad in their layers.

Jacob was glad he had reinstated the maid. Without her, the room might have been thick with frost. Even so, the chill lingered, and they pulled their chairs as close to the flames as possible.

Neither had spoken of Abby's brother on the journey home; both had remained all but silent, turning over aspects of the investigation.

Rubbing his hands together for warmth, Jacob voiced what they were both wondering: "Who is our murderer?"

Abby opened her satchel. "Let's spread our evidence before the fire, and pray it leads somewhere. Dirk de Vries's note must have dried by now."

Laid out on a cloth were: the two printed cards, de Vries's folded note, and the engraved amber bead Pepys had snatched from the murderer.

Jacob picked out the cards. Each bore a number beside a symbolic flame, which Abby's brother had claimed was his mark of trade: the flame of the rising Phoenix.

William had admitted to printing it, which marked him out as a suspect, though neither inquisitor could quite bring themselves to say it aloud. That he claimed to have no memory of the man who commissioned it only deepened their suspicions.

The first card, Mr Pepys had discovered on his person, placed there by his assailant on that first night of the Frost Fair. It seemed highly likely - if not certain - that he had been the intended target, particularly given the blackguard's howl of outrage when de Vries had perished instead.

Yet, inescapably, Pepys remained very much alive.

As did – for now, at least – the recipient of the second card: Signor Napoli.

His card had been secreted among his belongings. Why?

Jacob replaced the Number 2 card on the floor. "If neither Pepys nor Napoli is dead – praise the Lord – then perhaps the purpose of these cards is not as we believe?"

Abby handed Jacob de Vries's note. "Even if our deductions are awry, what's the meaning of the sequence? And who will receive the card numbered '3'?"

The folded paper found by the constable, once sodden by the Thames, then frozen, had now been fully dried before the fire. Rippled and degraded, it began to tear in Jacob's clumsy fingers as he attempted to tease it apart.

Abby retrieved it from him and, with patience, worked at the folds until it lay open.

Holes gaped where the water had eaten through, and whatever message had once been written there was all but lost, the ink having bled away into nothing.

Abby pieced together the remaining letters in her notebook:

…warn…
…ike at t… 30 Dece…
…ce shall cr… the Ki… all f…
…clear of the f…

As she held it up for Jacob to read, she noticed her hand tremble with anticipation. Despite all that was left of that first line, it told them all they needed to know.

A warning.

Was it a penned by de Vries, intended for another? Or a warning handed to the Dutchman?

And what did it foretell?

"What words end in '…ike'?" Abby asked, idly tickling her nose with her quill.

"Hike? Pike? Spike?"

"Strike!" She wrote it down. "It has to be. Someone will strike at… something…"

"On the 30th day of September?"

Thus, they began piecing together the Dutchman's note.

Be warned / A warning
We / I strike at t… on 30 December
…ce shall cr… the King shall f…
…clear of the f…

The full text of the third line continued to elude them, until Jacob suggested, simply, "So many words end in '…ce', yet is ours not the most likely of them all? 'Ice'?"

She almost hugged him. "And what does ice do? It cracks, Jacob!"

The ice shall crack and the King shall f…

"Nay," he murmured. "Surely, it cannot be."

The ice shall crack and the King shall fall

"And if that's so," she said, quelling her rising concern, "then the warning is clear."

Stay clear of the fair

With that in place, the second line grimly resolved itself. The puppeteer's Royal Command Performance, before the King himself, was scheduled for ten of the clock on the 30th day of December.

Thus, in their estimation, the full note read:

Be warned / A warning
We / I strike at ten of the clock on 30 December
The ice shall crack and the King shall fall
Stay clear of the fair

They stared at the page for some time, sombre and fearful.

At length, Jacob broke the silence. "We must warn the King."

"I'm going nowhere near that man."

After their previous investigation, Abby knew how dangerous he could be - and how his word meant nought.

Pursing his lips, Jacob nodded. "Aye. We must ask Mr Pepys… Fie!" He slapped his forehead. "He has navy business and will not be at the fair."

"Fear not, we'll track him down." She glanced at the amber bead. "I wonder, who is this 'R.F.', who seems to be behind all this? And how will he crack the ice, when 'tis strong enough to carry all those people?"

"I dread to think. You suspected an organisation, not one man?"

She rubbed her eyes, drained. "Whoever or whatever he is, he enjoys playing games."

"Aye, he toys with us, as Napoli plays with his puppets."

His words jolted her. "You speak of puppetry… something niggles at the back of my mind. Remember what Mr Pepys told us, about the night he was attacked?"

She recounted how Pepys had been practically pushed out of Tobias Mortimer's house by the host, and handed a lantern as he left. And how, when he arrived at Temple Stairs, a stranger had appeared, advising him to skirt Temple Street to avoid the crowds.

"Don't you find it suspicious?" she said. "A lantern will light your way - but it also picks you out when all around is dark and shrouded in mist."

Jacob said nothing.

"Is it not too convenient?" she persisted. "A strange man appears and steers Mr Pepys toward his waiting assailant? Had he taken Temple Street, the attack could ne'er have happened. 'Twas an ambush."

"Perhaps." Jacob massaged his chin. "But… do you suggest Sir Tobias Mortimer, an honourable Member of Parliament, is complicit? In murder?"

"You hold politicians in too high esteem, Jacob. Remember Culpepper and Davenport?" she asked, recalling their earlier investigation in London's coffee houses. "Tobias Mortimer was an ally of Matthew Hopkins. Men like that are the enemies of free thought."

"I cannot countenance it," he replied wearily. "It strikes at the very heart of our nation."

Chapter Twenty-Eight

Warmth

Despite Jacob's reservations, they agreed it was vital to track down Tobias Mortimer. Since neither had a clue to his whereabouts, they resolved to consult with Pepys.

Jacob insisted they not lose sight of other potential suspects. "The waterman, Hobbes, is an underhand knave with contempt in his eyes. Nor would I put murder past his associate, Carter." He paused. "And we are yet to question the Lottery man, whose wheel bore the words 'Rota Fortunae', and thus the letters 'R.F.'"

"Forget Sprig," she told him bluntly. "He's not our man."

"How can you be so sure?"

"When he rolled up his sleeves to fight Duke Hobbes…?" She waited, head cocked. "He wore no amber bead."

He groaned. "I should have noticed it myself."

A gust of wind rattled the windows.

"You can't see everything, Jacob."

His gaze lifted to the portraits of his family, their expressions aloof and reproachful.

Abby noticed, but said nothing - she could guess his thoughts.

For the first time, he detected the ghost of a smile on his younger sister Anne's lips.

"We can't choose our families," Abby said quietly.

He glanced at her and managed a smile - he knew her mind almost as well as she knew his. "Fear not," he said. "I shall interrogate your brother for you."

Though Jacob longed for sleep, it would not come. The chill outside crept in through every tiny crevice - and they were manifold - inhabiting the house like a stern matriarch.

His maid had placed a warming pan beneath the covers, but he and Abby had talked so long that the coals had long since gone cold.

The church bells chimed once, then, as he lay awake, twice. The timbers of the old house shuddered and groaned as he curled into a ball, willing the night away.

Then suddenly, his door creaked open.

Before he could react, Abby's voice called softly through the darkness. "'Tis only me, Jacob."

He poked his head out, gripping the blankets to his chin. "W...what do you want?"

"I'm freezing."

He felt her tug at the covers, trying to climb in beside him.

"Odd's fish, Abigail!" He sat bolt upright. "What manner of madness is this?"

She tugged again, and he abandoned the fight, scuttling toward the window.

Gratefully, she buried herself in the lingering warmth.

"It goes against all common decency!" he hissed in the darkness.

"What does?"

"Sleeping… in the same bed."

"But 'tis freezing."

She could hear his teeth chattering.

Eventually, and with great reluctance - having first offered to sleep in her bed, which she pointed out defeated the object of the arrangement - Jacob was coaxed in beside her. She had to swear never to breathe a word of their indiscretion to another soul, and was to lie as far from him as possible, facing outwards.

For some time, as he continued to lie awake, the mattress juddered in time with their shivers. Then he heard her shifting, followed by the sensation of her hand on his shoulder.

He tensed, eyes wide in the charged gloom.

When she sidled in behind him, her stomach against his shirted back, the warmth was so welcome he had to suppress a moan of contentment.

He lay motionless, scarcely daring to breathe, as her arm slipped around him and pulled him close.

Both inquisitors shivered, not from the cold, but from sheer, blissful relief.

Wallowing there, it struck him that he had not shared a bed with a woman for… in truth, a long time. He missed it. The comfort of Abby at his back only sharpened the loneliness that stalked his waking hours.

She was good to him - more patient than any living soul before her.

Bright, too. People like that tended to give him a wide berth. Yet she… she embraced his foibles.

Oh, and she was handsome! Though it never seemed to occur to her. She could have any man she wanted… were it not for her station in life.

I would be proud to call her my wife! he thought, then dismissed it at once.

They were inquisitors, bound by duty, and duty alone.

But such duty! The adventures they had shared! (Mr Pepys appeared in his mind, and he nudged him firmly aside.)

How fond they had grown of each another. Even he could accept that the feeling was mutual.

Did he love her, perhaps?

As a friend, certainly. Anything more would be… presumptuous.

Might she at least find me handsome in return?

A snort escaped him, as he pictured his reflection in a looking glass.

He fidgeted, then lay still, alert for any movement. None came. Her arm remained warm and soft across his chest.

But what if…?

What if her fondness for him had deepened, given all they had shared? Enough to see past his ungainly manner and unenviable features?

He remembered her skipping gaily before him on the path to Ravenscourt Manor, already at ease in his company, even in those early days of their investigations.

He thought of how readily now she would take his hands in hers.

Turning his head slightly towards her, he murmured, "Abby?"

Nothing.

A little louder. "Abby?"

Snuffling, she shifted against his back, and began lightly snoring.

Chapter Twenty-Nine

The Drum Boat

Abby was long up by the time Jacob stirred, and called upstairs when she heard him rising. "Hurry, Jacob - the King's life is in our hands."

When he joined her for breakfast, she shoved a bread roll at him.

Mr Pepys held the key, she said. They needed him to warn the King, and to divulge Tobias Mortimer's whereabouts. Yet they dared not risk wasting time travelling to Seething Lane, when he would likely be away on business.

"We have leeway," Jacob said. "The Royal Command Performance is not until the morrow."

"Aye," she replied, pulling on a glove. "Which is why we should return to the fair. I'd like to ride the drum boat."

He squinted. "For pleasure? At a time such as this?"

Shooting him a knowing glance, she made for the door.

The third full day of the Frost Fair found festivities in full swing.

As Abby and Jacob arrived at Temple Stairs, they watched two coaches, each drawn by four horses, racing across the ice toward London Bridge. More horses than ever roamed the frozen river, some ridden by a solitary gentleman, others harnessed to boats and sleds of varying sizes. Hackney coachmen, too, had taken to the ice.

One curious craft – a boat drawn by neither horse nor man, yet gliding along seemingly unpowered – flummoxed them both. They would later learn it was driven by an ingenious spring mechanism.

Out west, near the bend in the river at Westminster, they spied tiny figures of men and hounds in pursuit of a fox. "Such a spiriting sight!" Jacob exclaimed.

"Not if you're the fox," she countered.

He stared at her, bewildered. "But I am not the fox, and never shall be!"

"Have you ne'er felt hounded?"

That silenced him.

At the bottom of the steps, having inched forward in a tortuously slow line of shuffling people, one sound rose above all others: the rhythmic pounding of a drum, drawing steadily closer.

Doomp… Doomp… Doomp…

"The drum boat," said Jacob.

Abby had seen it the previous day, with Carter at the prow, banging its booming drum.

"Look!" Jacob said, pointing as the vessel loomed into view, pulled by four watermen heaving on a thick rope. "The drummer is Horatio Carter."

"Aye," she said, stepping onto the ice.

The exhausted watermen dropped the rope and sank to their knees in clouds of billowing breath. A rope ladder was dropped over the gunwale for passengers to disembark.

"Come," said Abby to Jacob, joining the line of Londoners eager to make the return journey to Southwark.

A canvas awning stretched over a curved wooden frame shielded the rear half of the boat from the elements. Abby and Jacob squeezed onto one of the benches nearest the front, shifting to make room for others. The excited chatter suggested this was a rare treat.

Ahead, Carter adjusted the drum slung around his neck, watching as the boat filled. When he caught the inquisitors' gaze, he showed not a flicker of recognition.

Another waterman, sneezing and coughing, trudged from row to row, collecting fares.

"Thruppence," he told Jacob, holding out a quivering hand.

Jacob frowned. "The last time I crossed the river, I paid a penny."

The old waterman sneezed. "Thruppence," he repeated.

Jacob closed his purse.

"If yer don't like it, orf yer go," the waterman said, jerking his thumb toward the ladder. "There's plenty more'll take yer place."

Abby nudged Jacob. "Just pay him."

She turned to view the people behind - hunched and bedraggled Londoners: children, parents, grandparents - faces weatherbeaten, eyes sunken, seeking a moment's solace from their upended lives.

Most can barely afford this, she thought.

When Carter banged his drum, the unseen men at the rope below groaned aloud.

He struck again; the boat lurched sideways, sending neighbour toppling into neighbour. Laughter rippled through the passengers as they righted themselves, muttering apologies.

Slowly, the boat swivelled, turning to face the opposite direction before setting off towards the south bank of the Thames.

Carter began beating his drum, slowly, methodically.

Doomp... Doomp... Doomp...

Lifted above the ice, the Frost Fair became a spectacle anew. They could see over the booths on Temple Street, all the way downriver to the bridge.

Abby leaned over the gunwale, marvelling at the novelty of gliding past the tops of so many heads. So many lives, she thought, unfolding below, swarming across the frozen river.

But there were weightier matters on her mind.

Motioning for Jacob to follow, she made her way to the prow.

He knew better than to ask why.

"Wha' d'you want?" Carter muttered, eyes fixed ahead.

When Jacob joined them, standing on Carter's other side, the drummer glanced between them." Be seated, would you. 'Tis not..."

"Tell me about Duke Hobbes," Abby cut in. "He seems a good man, despite outward appearances."

He cast her a glance. "Aye," he replied, wary. "That he is."

"He helped that poor woman yesterday, the one sheltering in the broken booth..."

Carter's bony jaw clenched. "What of it?"

"You did not."

His drumbeat faltered. "I've no need to answer to you." *Doomp.* "Duke... Mr Hobbes lost his family. Years ago, so 'tis told." *Doomp*. "Never speaks of it, but we watermen know. He…"

"What was your business with the Dutchmen?"

He stared at her. *Doomp*. "What Dutchmen?"

"The skaters. You spoke with them on the first day. We saw you."

Doomp. "They've gone. What of it?"

Doomp. "I believe they may be dangerous men."

Doomp. Carter snorted, but it lacked conviction. "Just 'cos they're Dutch…"

Doomp. "Nay, more than that. What was your business…" *Doomp*. "…with them?"

Doomp. The waterman said nothing, but shifted his feet.

Doomp. Doomp. Doomp.

"Your drum beats as fast as your heart, Mr Carter," Abby said, turning back to her seat and motioning for Jacob to follow.

Jacob was wide-eyed as they took their seats. "What was…?"

He was interrupted by a wail of anguish coming from the south bank, near the bend in the river.

Startled, Abby and Jacob stared at one another.

They had recognised the voice.

It was Mr Pepys's.

Chapter Thirty

Under Ice

"Take us there!" Abby ordered, pointing toward a figure in crimson, standing motionless and staring into the frozen shallows, while others hurried to join him. It was some way off, upriver toward Westminster, along the Southwark bank.

"We've reached our alighting point!" Carter called back, gesturing at towering Barge House ahead.

"Nay, take us there!" came the cry from one passenger. Then another.

"Aye, take us further!" added a third.

Carter shrugged and leaned over the prow. "That way, lads!"

Once again, groans rang out from the men at the ropes.

As the inquisitors had feared, the source of the guttural wail was indeed their employer, Mr Pepys. They disembarked quickly, watched with straining necks by the other passengers.

Approaching, they called out Pepys's name, and he turned, throwing up his hands.

"Look!" Pepys cried, pointing.

At the bottom of a steep, muddy bank, a tangle of thick, gnarled roots rose from the frozen surface of the river. The opaque, pale ice darkened near the bank, glistening where it had thinned and threatened to melt.

Among the roots, frozen detritus had gathered - an old bucket, an animal bone, a torn length of orange cloth - all trapped in the ice, jutting out at odd angles.

But there was something else down there.

Something large, shimmering white beneath a thin layer of ice.

All those gathered stared in eerie silence.

Peering closer, Abby saw what it was: a man's body, lying on its back, features distorted.

She knew him at once.

The white shirt and breeches, the raven-black hair.

She felt Jacob's reassuring presence at her back.

"Napoli," he murmured. "As the second card foretold."

"It makes no sense," she said.

Chapter Thirty-One

We Ended Him

The inquisitors had so many questions, yet no time to ask them.

"Oh my," gasped the constable, Archibald Frith, arriving on the scene. "Poor fellow."

A murmur of sympathy rose.

"Who found him?" Frith asked.

All fingers pointed to Pepys. "He did!"

Pepys could only bury his head in his hands.

The river was shallow, and Frith, stepping gingerly onto the ice, broke through with ease. A collective gasp followed as he straddled the body, knee deep in the chill brackish water, and exposed the puppeteer's neck. There, amid the ivory flesh, was a thin slit, no more than an inch wide. When he heaved poor Napoli over, there was an identical mark on the opposite side. Some fled at the sight.

"Looks like that's what did for him," said Frith.

Jacob waded into the frigid shallows and crouched to study the wound. "A narrow blade," he said, twisting Napoli's head so Abby could see clearly. "Perhaps a sword?"

Frith leaned in. "Too narrow."

"This was foretold by the murderer's card," Abby said.

"The same card your brother printed." The words were out before Jacob could stop them.

A hush fell, and all eyes turned to Abby.

"If there's something you've not told…" Frith began, but Jacob cut him off.

"Hold!" the inquisitor cried, raising an arm. "There is something in…" Prizing open the puppeteer's clenched fist, he drew out a small parcel wrapped in waxed cloth. "…his hand."

Pepys cleared his throat, shuffling uncomfortably. "Constable, this is the scene of a crime. Would you move these people on?"

Though one or two bystanders lingered obstinately, the inquisitors, Pepys and Frith were able to confer in low voices.

Jacob unwrapped the parcel to reveal a folded piece of parchment. When he opened it, the constable almost choked.

You applauded this fool, thus we ended him.

Will you defend his honour, coward King?
Face us on the morrow at ten.
We shall watch his ghost perform for you.
— R.F.

"Oh my," said Frith. "What can it mean?"

It was perfectly clear to Abby and Jacob. The devilish organisation known only as 'R.F.' had murdered Napoli to draw Charles to the ice.

Coward King, indeed.

Abby fumbled in her satchel. "You mustn't allow His Majesty to rise to this." She thrust the tattered Dutchman's note into Frith's hand. "Something terrible is planned here."

To her dismay, he began to chuckle. "What is this? Meaningless letters? Is it some sort of code?"

When she produced her notebook, showing their attempted solution, he only laughed harder. "This is fanciful nonsense, mistress!"

"Nay, Mr Frith," she protested. "His Majesty's life is in grave danger. That note is the one..."

Frith shook his head, lips pursed. "See here, this third line..." He pointed.

...ce shall cr... the Ki... all f...

"You claim it reads, 'The ice shall crack and the King shall fall.'?"

"Aye." She studied his gaze, frowning.

"It might also read…" Frith paused, tapping his nose. "It might also read, 'Grace shall crown the King, all faithful rejoice!'" He grinned, pleased with himself.

Pushing Abby aside, Jacob stepped forward. "Sir, this is no laughing matter. We believe this threat to be deadly serious."

"Mr…?"

Jacob sighed. "Standish."

"Mr Standish. I have here two notes. One, clearly addressed to the King himself by this 'R.F.' fellow, which I am duty bound to deliver at once to His Majesty. The other…" He waved the Dutchman's note airily, allowing it to fall to the ice. "A jumble of nonsense that would see me flogged were I to present it at court."

With that, he turned on his heel and scuttled away.

Chapter Thirty-Two

A Fresh Clue

Pepys and his inquisitors stood in bewildered silence as men arrived to extract the puppeteer from his icy tomb.

"You believe His Majesty's life is in mortal peril?" Pepys asked Abby.

When she nodded grimly, he hung his head.

"What drew you here, sir," she asked, "when you told us you had business elsewhere?"

Pepys scratched beneath his periwig and sighed. "Last night, while we took supper at The Horn, a boy accosted me. He said I had been seen when the Dutchman fell, and that I was to come to the south bank this very morning, where Southwark meets Lambeth. There, I would find orange cloth at the water's edge." He gestured toward the scrap caught in the roots.

As they looked, Napoli was being plucked from the river, a haunted expression etched on his face.

"I could not help but see… him," Pepys concluded.

"Sir," said Jacob, "we have assured you many times, de Vries's death was not your doing."

"Yet somebody witnessed it, Jacob. What choice had I, but to yield to their blackmail? And now… it leads me to a second death." He shook his head mournfully. "Why me?"

"For somebody's amusement," Abby said, turning to Jacob. "Our puppet master strikes again."

She explained the inquisitors' theory, that Pepys had been manipulated on the night of de Vries's death, first hastened to the river, then guided to skirt Temple Street, rather than walk along it.

"But…" Pepys looked aghast. "The man who insisted I leave for the fair was… Surely you cannot mean…?"

Abby raised an eyebrow.

"Sir Tobias Mortimer?" Pepys exclaimed. "Member of Parliament for Rye in Sussex, staunch defender of English trade and moral order…?"

Jacob nodded.

"…Is behind this treason? A plot to assassinate the King?" Pepys blinked a few times. "But the masked knave who pushed me that night… He was half Mortimer's size."

"I'm not suggesting Mortimer's the murderer, sir," Abby said. "But I fear he pulls the strings."

"Ne'er have I heard such nonsense! A distinguished Member of Parliament!" He turned on Jacob. "Should we not be visiting the oaf Sprig at his Lottery Booth. His Wheel of Fortune bore the legend…"

Jacob avoided his employer's gaze. "These murders run deeper and darker, sir, than a craven old man fleecing pennies from the poor."

Pepys spluttered. "And you believe Sir Tobias responsible, Abigail?"

"I do, sir."

Pepys turned to Jacob. "Do you concur?"

"There is one other thing…" Opening his coat, Jacob pulled an old tool from his belt.

"What is it?" Abby asked.

"I found it beside the puppeteer's body and secreted it about my person, fearing Frith might confiscate it." He turned it over in his hand. "A chisel."

Abby almost snatched it from him. "Why didn't you show me this sooner? Did the murderer use this to break through the ice, then place Napoli's body there, leaving the river to freeze over him?" She paused, peering. "Hold, I see marks scratched here…"

Jacob took it back. The chisel was ten inches long, its sodden wooden handle bound in worn leather. On the end of the cylindrical handle there were indeed letters scratched… "'M.H.'" said Jacob.

"M.H.?" said Pepys. "Who could it be?"

"Certainly not Tobias Mortimer," Pepys interjected.

Their minds turned, before Jacob sucked in a breath. "Is Duke not Marmaduke by another name?"

"Marmaduke Hobbes." Pepys folded his arms. "That ghastly waterman."

Where did it leave them?

Even as their noses stung with cold and the bitter wind cut through their layers, they lingered out on the exposed stretch of river, debating their next move.

Now they had two bodies: de Vries and Napoli, Dutchman and Italian. If they were indeed the intended victims, and not Pepys and Napoli, then the obvious motive lay in hatred and distrust of foreigners.

Many an Englishman harboured such prejudice, Pepys pointed out. What other reason could there be?

"Did Hobbes hold such a prejudice?" Jacob wondered aloud.

Pepys laughed wryly. "He is a Thames waterman, Jacob!"

Abby blew into her cupped hands and rubbed them briskly together. "Hobbes's colleague, Carter, speaks highly of him. He seems to care only for his men and their livelihoods - livelihoods dependent on this fair. Surely, men's deaths can only drive people away?" She looked earnestly to Pepys. "We should meet with Mortimer, sir.

I still believe a man of power lies at the heart of these murders."

"Even if 'tis Mortimer, he would ne'er grant you an audience!"

"Aye, sir. But he would you."

Chapter Thirty-Three

The Hourglass

I t took some persuading.

Pepys was no friend of Mortimer, though the Sussex MP carried enough weight in naval circles to be kept on-side.

"A Puritan bore," Pepys called him, "his discourse mired in biblical allusions. He bears a perpetual air of disapproval."

The borough of Rye, which Mortimer represented in Parliament, was a key port on the south coast. It granted him influence in naval affairs, ensuring that he and Pepys crossed paths on occasion. Their first meeting had been at a supper hosted by Sir William Penn, Commissioner of the Navy Board and a close associate of Pepys.

Mortimer had held court - despite refusing the wine - expounding on the Dutch threat and the navy's chronic underfunding, before launching into a sermon on moral decay and the perils of attending stage plays.

"Only the previous night, I had attended James Shirley's The Court Secret with my wife," Pepys recalled. "I confess, she deemed it the worst play she had ever seen."

All three breathed a sigh of relief as they climbed Temple Stairs and set off up Middle Temple Lane. The appeal of the Frost Fair was waning.

To their right lay an area of woodland, frequented on sunny days by the lawyers of the Inns of Court - Jacob often waved to them, and often they ignored him.

But these were not sunny days, and the trees stood desolate, crusted in hoar frost, rising like the dead from the ground.

Pepys stopped outside an arched door set within a high-walled forecourt. "Well, here we are," he said, stamping his feet. "Against my better judgment. What, precisely, do you expect to discover?"

"The mark of the man," Abby replied, pushing open the door.

Inside, beyond a lawn of undulating white, was a tall, red-brick building, its entrance framed by ornate stone columns. The steep roof had shed a slab of thick snow, which now hung precariously over the eaves, exposing a wide area of dull lead.

Beside each column sat a stone lion crowned with a hat of snow. Fierce, open-jawed and sharp-toothed, they seemed to be roaring at the iniquities of the world.

A liveried servant answered the door. Recognising Pepys from the recent dinner party, he bade them enter and inquired after their business. Pepys, as instructed, lied that he had an appointment with Sir Tobias.

Abby wished to catch Mortimer unawares.

She had planned a surprise - but received one instead.

As they approached Mortimer's study, led by the servant, the door flew open and a lady bustled out, dressed in the most expensive finery. At the sight of Abby and Jacob, she stopped dead and her mouth fell open.

They each recognised one another instantly.

The lady was Arabella Wyndham, the King's courtier.

"What the…?" Abby managed, startled.

As swiftly as Arabella's composure had deserted her, so it returned.

With her nose in the air and a cursory nod to Pepys, she brushed past the little group and made for the exit.

There was no time to react, as the servant opened Mortimer's study door and announced their arrival.

Mortimer shot to his feet. "What in God's providence?" he thundered, jowls quivering. Then his piggy eyes settled on Pepys. "*Mr Pepys?* What brings you…?" His gaze shifted. "And who…?"

In a deft movement, his hand slid something beneath a Bible on his desk - not deft enough, however, since they all saw it.

The servant, realising he had been duped, began babbling apologies. Mortimer drove him from the room before sinking back into his chair.

Sir Tobias was a large, imposing man in a sheepskin-lined coat, seated at a desk. Its only adornments were the well-thumbed Bible, some paperwork, a carved wooden box, a candlestick and an hourglass. Religious texts lined the walls, their dark bindings soaking up the scant lighting. The room was joyless.

"Forgive my impertinence at this hour, Sir Tobias," Pepys began, "however, I…"

He had a story prepared – advice on a petition concerning naval provisions in Rye – but Mortimer seemed more interested in the inquisitors. His right eyelid twitched as he squinted at them, his breath thick and rasping. "Are these…?"

"These are my inquisitors, Sir Tobias," Pepys said. "Jacob Standish and Abigail Harcourt."

Jacob and Abby bowed.

"Where is this young woman's chaperone?" Mortimer asked. Though his tone was measured, his demeanour suggested otherwise.

When Abby stepped forward, the men instinctively did the same. "Sir, I…"

"Silence!" he bellowed. "Thou shalt not speak in the presence of men! 'I suffer not a woman to teach, nor to usurp authority over the man, but to be in silence.'"

Pepys, who recognised the passage but could not place it, heard himself emit an exasperated sigh.

Mortimer turned on him. "I smell deceit in the air, Mr Pepys. Pray, tell me, what is the reason for this unexpected pleasure?"

Pepys considered himself a confident fellow, skilled in public speaking and unshaken in the company of power. Yet even he found himself faltering as he spun his fictitious tale. The longer he spoke, the flimsier it felt.

Meanwhile, with Mortimer distracted, Abby dropped to one knee, feigning an adjustment to her stocking.

When she rose, she had shuffled closer to Mortimer, within a foot or two of his desk. Noticing it, his glare shifted from Pepys to Abby.

Before he could speak, she reached out and snatched up the hourglass.

"What's this, Sir Tobias?" she asked, though she knew full well.

Examining it perfunctorily, she upended it, setting the sand in motion, then tossed it to Jacob. "What do you make of it?" she asked.

What followed seemed to unfold in slow motion.

Sir Tobias's mouth gaped open, teeth bared, resembling one of his stone lions, as he prepared to unleash his wrath. Pepys, focussed on maintaining his elaborate fiction, only prattled on, oblivious.

Jacob, meanwhile, saw too late what Abby had done. Emitting a high-pitched, strangled noise, he thrust out his hands toward the tumbling hourglass.

As Abby had hoped, he did not catch it.

The hourglass bounced from his grasp, struck the edge of Mortimer's desk, miraculously survived, then tumbled to the wooden floor. There, it duly shattered, scattering shards of glass in every direction.

Abby threw up her arms in mock horror, while Mortimer froze.

The next instant, Jacob was on his hands and knees beneath the desk, sweeping at the fragments with his sleeve, blathering apologies.

"Leave it be, you blundering clod! Leave it be!" Mortimer bellowed, dropping to the floor to attend to the mess at the opposite end of the desk.

Seizing her moment, Abby lifted the Bible and slid the hidden paper into her hand. Pepys, watching in mute bewilderment, could not decide whether to chastise or applaud. He settled, fortunately, for neither.

As Abby stepped back, Mortimer's head rose from behind the desk, gimlet eyes blazing, just as Jacob plucked a vicious-looking shard from his palm.

Lips curled in silent outrage, the Member of Parliament for Sussex pointed to the door.

"Quite so," said Pepys, bowing. "I think it best that we..." His voice trailed off.

"I know what you did," Mortimer growled, as Abby was about to leave.

Composing herself, she turned. "I beg your pardon, sir?"

He smiled a hateful smile. "You shall beg for more than my pardon, harlot, ere our time together is passed."

Chapter Thirty-Four

The Blaze Eternal

"Abigail Harcourt!" Pepys declared, once they were safely outside. "Had I not witnessed it with my own eyes! Your bravado and cunning are beyond words. Indeed, I find myself at a loss, for once."

Jacob, head down and sullen, kicked at a snowdrift. "She made me look a fool."

"Jacob!" she cajoled, slapping him heartily on the back. "'Twas merely a ruse, devised on the spur of the moment. And it worked!"

Grinning, she produced the piece of paper so deviously purloined from Mortimer's desk.

"I do not wish to be your stooge," Jacob muttered.

But she could see him eyeing her prize.

Pepys, too. "What is writ there?" he urged.

"Aye," said Jacob, taking it. "What is writ here?"

Brethren of the Righteous Flame
We assemble at Barge House
30 December at eight of the morning

The Righteous Flame Shall Blaze Eternal

Their intakes of breath sucked in the chill.

"We have our answer," said Jacob. "R.F. is the Righteous Flame - and they meet on the morrow."

Pepys threw up his hands. "Will somebody please explain…?"

"Sir, your assailant wore the amber bead, signifying his attachment to this Righteous Flame," said Jacob, "an organisation to which Sir Tobias, we now discover, is connected."

Abby took the paper back. "He knew I stole this, he told me so - yet he allowed it…"

"It would seem you were right, Abigail," said Pepys. "Sir Tobias Mortimer may indeed be a danger to His Majesty, and I shudder to think where his subterfuge ends."

"And what part Arabella Wyndham may play in it," Abby added.

Jacob straightened his periwig. "Aye, but what can we do?"

"We, Mr Standish," said Pepys, "can return to the warmth of Seething Lane, where we may plot in comfort. If ne'er I see snow again, it will be too soon."

Chapter Thirty-Five

Aulay's Return

A ulay Cussell could have hanged on Thomas Langridge's word, which was good enough for the local magistrate. Langridge toyed with him, let him rot in Newgate jail for a year or two, then eventually grew bored. When sentencing came, with a devious smirk, he requested Aulay's life be spared.

Instead of the gallows, the young Scotsman was transported to Barbados, indentured to seven years of servitude on a sugar plantation.

Aulay had never even heard of Barbados.

When he had imagined escaping England's shores, the destinations had been nameless, conjured from a boy's longing for adventure. He would learn to fear this one.

The journey alone almost killed him. Packed below decks like bodies in a plague pit, he and his fellow convicts endured fetid air, pitiful rations and outbreaks of disease that swept through the vessel.

By the time they staggered onto land in Bridgeton, shielding their eyes from the relentless sun, almost a third of those who had boarded in London were gone - lost to the sea, nameless and unmourned.

Aulay was distraught. A place could not have felt more distant from his precious Scotland - the homeland he now longed to return to. The air burned like a furnace and the land seemed alive with scaled creatures lifted from a twisted demonology.

He was sent to work on the sugar-cane plantation of Marcus Powell, a hard-nosed Englishman who had arrived in Barbados a decade earlier and built his wealth through tobacco.

At first, the relentless toil nearly broke him. The sun seemed never to set, the cane leaves sliced at his arms, and the overseers drove them like carthorses.

But Aulay was no fool. He saw men crushed by their labour, and he saw men who found ways to ease their suffering. If Jim Quigley had taught him anything, it was that fortune favoured the cunning.

He befriended Jonas Finch, a sailor-turned-farrier who, once the fields had emptied, was put to work in the forge, crafting tools, shoeing horses and repairing plantation equipment. One night, Aulay was assigned to assist him.

That bond probably saved his life. It gave him someone to laugh with, and a reason to endure.

Finch, like Aulay, was something of a rogue. Using makeshift equipment, he had managed to brew a hellish liquor from fermented molasses, which burned their throats and addled their minds. Together, they smuggled jars past the overseers, bartering them for pathetic luxuries - a twist of tobacco, a sliver of salted fish, a dented spoon.

One awful night, years into Aulay's servitude, they were caught with a flagon of their contraband. Hauled before Powell, Aulay and Finch were flogged without mercy, and when at last the punishment ended, their indenture terms were prolonged - indefinitely, it seemed.

"I'll keep you vermin here till your final gasp," Powell promised.

Finch's, sadly, was not far off. Whether it was old age - he was 46 or 47, perhaps 48; he could no longer recall - or the effects of the labour on his battered body, it was impossible to say. Most likely, it was both.

Aulay buried his friend in the baked earth, digging the grave with his bare hands in a forgotten corner of the plantation. Finally defeated, he resigned himself to seeing out his days in servitude.

But fate had other plans. Powell died first, early in 1666.

Seized by hope and the sliver of a chance, Aulay fled under cover of darkness, slipping down to the docks as the plantation descended into turmoil. There, he stowed away aboard an

English ship, bound for home after depositing its latest cargo of damned ne'er-do-wells.

It struck him that he had once dreamed of stowing away to a far-off land - yet fortune found him fleeing one.

Aulay Cussell arrived back in London an old man. Strange tufts of orange hair encircled his scalp and his skin was crinkled and leathery, like a well-used glove. His hands had become claw-like, from the years of cutting, bundling and lashing. He could no more have palmed a dice than conjure coins from curd.

He sought out Jim Quigley, naturally, and found their old tenement razed to the ground. His friend had not been seen around Whitechapel in years, he discovered.

"Last I heard tell, he was plying his trade Westminster way," one local told him.

He hobbled all the way to Hackney in search of his mother and sister, and, truth be told, was heartened not to find them. None of the women remembered them, even, and he prayed they had escaped to happiness.

Sheltering in the city's doorways, Aulay scraped by on menial jobs, earning farthings where he could. Though destitute, he found solace in people: passers-by he came to recognise, a few who stopped to talk. When he told them his tale, most scoffed and called him a liar.

He would nod and begin to wonder whether he had indeed imagined it all.

As winter set in, he found regular work delivering sea-coal - demand had risen with the cold, and the merchants needed extra hands.

At first, he welcomed the chill; it added weight to his meagre purse.

But then the snow came and would not stop.

His coat, damp by day, froze stiff by night. The watchmen, who once moved him along, took pity and left him be. Still, he could not sleep.

The ice became his bane. His footing, already unsure, turned treacherous. He took fall after fall, his knees bruised, his limbs aching, his fingers too numb to grip. The coal unbalanced him further, and if he fell and spilled it, children would appear from nowhere, to steal the precious lumps. What was lost, he had to repay.

Then came the Frost Fair of 1666.

It brought to mind his first frost fair, where he had met Jim Quigley, when his future had felt alive with possibilities. Now, so very many years later, he looked upon the same false carnival and saw it for what it was. No warmth, no wonder, only cold and cruel reality.

One night, shivering so violently he feared his very bones might break, he set down his sack. As he did so, he lost his balance.

His head cracked against the ice, and a burst of white light filled his vision. For an instant, he wondered if the Lord Himself were calling him to Heaven.

He lay there, listening to his own shallow, fitful breaths, feeling colder than he had ever felt before.

Beside him, a few lumps of coal had spilled from his sack.

If I light them, *he thought,* I can be warm.

He imagined it: the comforting, life-affirming glow. The warmth enveloping him, like a hug from his mother when he was a wee bairn.

Dare I? *he wondered.*

Aulay sat up.

Breaking the law had ruined him. It had cost him years of his life.

He had left all that deviance behind, and was proud of that. And yet…

A voice entered his tortured mind – a booming voice, as he imagined God might sound.

It spoke to him.

"Burn the coal and live," it said. "Or deliver it and die."

Chapter Thirty-Six

3

Jacob had hoped Pepys might suggest sleeping at his townhouse on Strand Lane, if only out of curiosity. It was considerably closer, for a start. The rooms were more spacious, the ceilings higher, the portraiture more expensive, and the fireplaces far grander than those of Pepys's grace-and-favour navy dwelling. Though Jacob only occupied Strand Lane by the favour of his otherwise distant mother, he took pride in its opulence.

But it was not to be. Pepys was a gentleman with home at his heart, and he insisted on paying for a hackney coach to Seething Lane.

The journey passed in silence, each occupant lost in thought, and, in one case, sulking.

Abby, for her part, had mixed feelings about Pepys's house. She had lived there for more than two years and was grateful for the roof over her head. Yet it was no home, not truly - not when she had been the servant.

The reminders had been constant: the interminable hours, the back-breaking drudgery, the lack of time to herself, always at another's beck and call. Pepys and his wife had grown increasingly civil as the months passed, yet she had endured seeing colleagues - friends - soundly thrashed by their master, whose temper was wont to boil over.

She knew every inch of the place, having dusted its corners and polished every crevice of its wood and metal - far more intimately, she imagined, than Pepys himself. In that respect, it felt familiar. And through familiarity had grown ease.

Abby and the kitchen maid, Mary Blythe, had formed a tight bond. They were of similar age, both from poor families, both orphaned, though Mary could neither read nor write.

There came a time, when the master and mistress were away, when they would emerge from their stations, like mice from their holes, and make merry.

In stolen moments of joy, the pair would pilfer sugared almonds, mimic the Pepyses and their guests with ridiculous accents and exaggerated bows, or whisper tales of ghostly apparitions to one another by candlelight, long after they should have been asleep.

One evening, emboldened by the empty house, they dared something more brazen. Mary, ever the more reckless of the two, had wagered Abby that she could not steal into her mistress's chamber and try on the French silk gown lately gifted to her by her husband.

A little wine, left over from the previous night's supper party, had played its part in Abby's acquiescence.

Laced tight inside the expensive bodice, she paraded around Elizabeth's chamber acting like a lady of court - to Betsy's tipsy cackles - until the distant slam of a door turned their amusement to horror.

With no time to remove the bodice, both women had raced up the servants' stairs then lay, hearts pounding, beneath their covers, praying their game was not discovered.

Abby managed to return the gown to its armoire while Elizabeth was sleeping, and became convinced she had escaped unnoticed.

Her delusion, however, proved short-lived.

Before noon, Pepys summoned her to his study. "I trust I need not ask why my wife's French silk gown was absent from its place last night?" he asked.

Her stomach dropped. What could she say? "Sir, I beg you, forgive me. I meant no harm."

"Meant no harm?" he repeated, eyeing her narrowly. "And yet, had my wife awoken and found it missing, I would have had no peace for a month."

A smile curled on his lips, and she silently exhaled.

"Foolishness, Abigail. Unforgivable foolishness. I expect better of you."

He had become fond of her, she realised.

Now that Abby was no longer Pepys's servant, her confidence had only grown. It was why, as she settled into an armchair that night, letting the fire's heat seep into her bones, she blithely kicked off one frozen shoe, then the other.

As she did so, something fell to the floor.

Jacob saw it too, and bent to retrieve it.

It was a small card, and all too familiar.

3 🔥

London: Printed on the ICE, on the River of Thames, December 27. 1666.

The room fell very silent as Jacob handed it to Pepys.

Mary Blythe's footsteps approached up the stairs. At the top, she opened her mouth to speak, then faltered at the tension in the room.

Involuntarily, Pepys shivered. "Mary," he said distractedly. "Did my delivery of sea-coal arrive this morning? Elizabeth informs me we are running low."

"Aye, sir. Mr Cussell brought it early. Terrible, he looked, poor man. He…"

"Indeed, indeed, enough of the unfortunate Mr Cassell." Pepys waved her away and turned back to Abby.

"You must remain here," he told her. "I shall summon marines for your protection."

Lost in thought, she stared into the fire. "Nay, sir. I'll not be cowed by Mortimer and the Righteous Flame. I wouldn't give them the satisfaction." She managed a smile. "Besides, we're your inquisitors."

"How did that card come to be in your shoe?" Jacob asked.

"While I was stealing the note from his desk, Mortimer was beneath it. He must have slipped it there." Abby poked the coals. "You have to admire his cunning."

"Yet I do not, Abigail," huffed Pepys. "The man is a scoundrel of the highest order. The King shall hear of his subversive organisation. Its members shall be rounded up and duly punished."

"But 'tis the King who is the true target of the villains, sir," she pointed out, catching his gaze. "Not I. My only crime is angering Mortimer. All the clues begin to make sense."

Abby outlined her theory.

Pepys, she said, had been the first intended victim. His assailant's anguished moan when de Vries fell through the ice suggested as much. Why anybody bore Pepys such malice, she could not say, but it would also explain his summoning to the site of Napoli's body.

"By good fortune," she added, "the constable does not - and will never, it seems - suspect you of murder."

"I should hope not!" Pepys exclaimed.

The Dutchmen, she went on, were in collusion with the Righteous Flame. The note found on de Vries warned of a coming catastrophe, which would rend the ice and kill the King. And it would occur on the morrow, at ten of the clock - the precise hour of the puppeteer's Royal Command Performance. "It can't be a coincidence."

Jacob screwed up his face. "Then why murder Napoli?"

"Mr Pepys told us His Majesty loathes the cold, and would ne'er attend an outdoor puppet show in such weather." She let it sink in. "But murder the puppeteer, mock the King for approving him, taunt him as a coward... He may be powerless to resist the lure of vengeance."

"All true, Abigail," said Pepys. "But 'twas you I told of His Majesty's disdain for ice - not the Righteous Flame. How could they possibly know?"

She had no answer.

Jacob spoke up. "And the Righteous Flame meet two hours prior to the performance."

"Aye," said Abby. "Their involvement is not for debate. I also believe Horatio Carter is inveigled, given his conference with the Dutchmen, but can't fathom why."

"But why, Abigail? Why murder His Majesty? 'Tis the direst of crimes, bringing to mind the dark days of the King's father." Pepys sighed deeply. "'Tis unimaginable."

"I fear your allusion to the days of King Charles I ring true, sir. The Righteous Flame, I believe, are Puritan men who long for a return to the days of Commonwealth. It may be that Arabella Wyndham's son, Henry, is their intended puppet ruler, with them at the strings. We know that mother and son crave the throne."

Pepys buried his face in his hands. "God help us. How are we to stop this despicable plan?"

"We must gamble, sir. I say we go after Mortimer."

At length, a plan was set out.

They would sleep at Seething Lane and wake at five, allowing ample time to prepare for what promised to be the young inquisitors' most perilous day in Pepys's employ.

With the Righteous Flame gathering at the abandoned Barge House in Southwark at eight, they would return to Temple Stairs by coach...

"What if agents of the Righteous Flame await us there?" Jacob pointed out. "Sir Tobias knows we are aware of the gathering."

Pepys nodded. "An excellent point, Jacob. Then I suggest we access the river at Blackfriars, where we are not expected."

"Still, I must visit Temple Street." Abby hesitated before adding, "I must speak with my brother. He printed each of those cards, one of which has now fallen to me."

Jacob's eyes widened. "Nay, Abby, let me…"

She shook her head. "I must face him myself. He shall answer for his part in this devilry."

Chapter Thirty-Seven

Flight

Jacob did not need Mary Blythe to rouse him at the appointed hour. He had slept only fitfully, his mind alive with anticipation, and had lain awake listening to the wind grow in ferocity. It rattled shutters and clattered latches, creating a demented, ghoulish symphony.

The weather was worsening.

Donning his many layers by the light of a single candle, he crept downstairs, careful not to wake the others. Excitement throbbed in his chest, which the dangers ahead only sharpened. Here was his chance to prove himself, to demonstrate his bravery.

When he shone his candle into the parlour, Pepys and Abby were already there, seated in silence, waiting patiently.

"Jacob," she said. "Your hat is on backwards."

Mary, already bustling in the kitchen, set out a loaf of coarse rye bread, a wedge of cheese and a jug of small ale.

These, she supplemented with a few cold cuts from an earlier supper. No feast, but it would suffice.

They were eager to begin.

The wind tore off both men's hats the moment they stepped outside. It whipped swirling snow into their faces, forcing them all to turn their backs.

"My goodness," said Pepys, raising his voice to be heard. "Perhaps the Righteous Flame will postpone their gathering?"

His inquisitors' expressions suggested otherwise.

At this early hour, and in such wretched conditions, Thames Street was all but deserted, leaving them no choice but to trudge the disconsolate mile to Blackfriars. The wind, at least, was at their backs, at one point almost lifting Abby off her feet.

Above them, thick cloud blanketed the sky, glowing silvery-white where it shrouded the moon. To their right, great plumes of powdered snow were flung into the air from the ruined city. To their left: the river.

The Thames was barren, a spine of ice, its only feature the distant thread of Temple Street. At the far end of those booths, barely visible through the swirling snow, stood the tall, ominous shape of Barge House.

So fierce was the wind that even Jacob lost his footing. Picking himself up without a word, he pressed on, one foot in front of the other.

"This may be what Hell is like," Pepys hollered into the gale.

When the sun rose at their backs, they scarcely noticed. The sky turned a shade lighter, and the pale orb - so pale it could barely be seen - climbed gradually over London Bridge.

At Blackfriars Stairs, feet somehow both numb and sore, they trod virgin snow down to the ice. Some drifts lay so deep they swallowed Abby's knees. Jaw clenched, she paid them no heed.

The wind bowled up the Thames, whipping up settled snow, billowing and battering the canvas of the booths, though the watermen's long-practised knots held firm.

"I understand now why some call it Freezeland Street," Jacob muttered to himself.

A hundred yards ahead, through the blizzard, lay Temple Stairs. They could make out grey, silhouetted figures there, some heading in, others hovering.

In the shelter of a jutting embankment, Abby motioned for them to stop. "I must speak with my brother alone," she said. "If agents of the Righteous Flame await us at Temple Stairs, we'd do well to take different routes to Barge House."

Pepys and Jacob should veer onto the Thames ice, she said, while she risked the well-trodden street of booths, where her brother was likely setting up for the day.

But neither man would hear of it.

A voice rose above the weather's din as the three approached Temple Stairs.

"The Almighty hath struck down the ungodly in your midst!" it cried. "Yet still ye cavort and gamble and mock His will! Turn away! Lest your name also be writ upon the ice in death!"

Puritan rantings, Abby thought. They had expected to encounter agents of the Righteous Flame – and there, no doubt, one stood.

Jacob brushed crusted snow from his eyebrows. "This foul weather will deter more folk than his preaching!"

Shouting to be heard, his words drew the preacher's attention. Dressed identically to the unsettling figure they had encountered with the placard – masked, in a hooded vermillion robe held tight with a drawstring – he called another man, identically dressed, to his side.

The two stood together, watching Pepys and his inquisitors battle onward.

"What is your business?" the preacher's companion called out when they drew near.

"What business is that of yours?" Jacob demanded, halting before him.

Pepys stepped alongside, while Abby held back. She recognised the mask at once. The same mask worn by the robed man with the placard. The deep-set eyes, the expressionless gaze.

The mask, she now realised, of the Righteous Flame.

They had reached the stairs. Tradesmen passed by, laden with goods for their booths, heads bowed into the gale. Hardy visitors mingled among them, undeterred by the conditions.

Church bells chimed the seventh hour.

"I teach the Lord's work," the preacher said, gesturing about him. "To these heathens, whose days shall end in the fires of Hell."

His voice was unfamiliar.

"If you are so proud of your work, preacher," said Jacob, "why hide behind a mask?"

The preacher's companion, a broader man, stepped forward. "We seek three persons. Two gentlemen and a lady - such as yourselves."

"For why?" Pepys asked, feigning innocence.

"For no reason, I assure you," the broad man replied, pausing. "*Mr Samuel Pepys.*"

Panicked, Pepys swivelled sharply and slipped on the ice. Down he went as the two adversaries pounced.

While Jacob hurled himself into the fray, Abby darted into Temple Street.

Chapter Thirty-Eight

Denial

At William Wrathbone's sign of the Phoenix, Abby stopped. Hands on hips, bending, she caught her breath. Glancing back up Temple Street, she was relieved to see no one following. The two men could look after themselves - she hoped.

A sideways glance caught her brother at work inside his booth, with a boy stacking paper off to one side. A dread sense settled in her stomach. So many questions, yet she feared the answers.

William had his back to her, leaning into his press. She watched as he froze, straightened - was he sniffing the air? - then, for no apparent reason, turned.

"Abby!" he cried in delight, running towards her.

Stony-faced, she raised a hand.

It stopped him in his tracks, his grin slipping. "May we discourse?" he asked.

"'Tis why I'm here, William."

The boy noticed them, and William motioned for him to continue his work.

"You were once our father's apprentice," she said. "Yet you forsook him in his hour of need, and now you forsake our family name, William Wrathbone.

When he stepped forward, she halted him again.

"What could I do?" he pleaded. "I…"

"Are you so cowardly, you cannot take responsibility for your own actions?"

He gazed at her imploringly. "Pray, sister, let me explain…"

She had heard it all before. The soldiers, the chest-beating, the supposed threats against his life.

Enduring the same sorry tale again only sickened her, and eventually she threw up her hands. "You signed a pact with the Devil, William."

He squinted, nonplussed. "The Devil?"

"Tobias Mortimer. The Righteous Flame. Puritan men."

"How did…?" He caught himself. She knew. Somehow, she always knew - she had always been a sharp one. William allowed himself a smile.

"Those are the men whose pamphlets you printed, condemning our father and good men like him. You struck a bargain with Mortimer and his cronies, to spare your own sorry life."

He avoided her gaze. "But I tore up that deal, Abigail. After you cast me aside, I cast Mortimer aside. I fell in with a kindly gentleman who patronised my printing work. He saw that I was lonely on Bleak Alley, and invited me to live with him and his family. We moved this year to Deptford, after…" He stopped and smiled. "I prattle on."

She knew he was lying about Mortimer, since he had printed the Righteous Flame's death cards. "After what? Who was this man?"

William gestured to his sign. "Hezekiah Wrathbone. I took his name in gratitude for his generosity."

She growled, unable to sort his lies from truth. "What does the Righteous Flame mean to you?" Her eyes flicked to her brother's hat. "You wear flame-coloured feathers. Do you call those men your brethren? Have you turned to their ways?"

He shook his head, a picture of innocence.

"When last we met," she went on, "you spoke of the Feast of Holy Innocents. You said, 'Anglicans know it as Childermas' - yet our family was Anglican."

"What of it?"

"Would you not have said, '*We* Anglicans…'? Has your faith turned?"

If she had caught him out, he disguised it well. "I told you, Abby, the flames signify my Phoenix, my mark of trade. I know nought of this Righteous Flame."

"You're lying. I've seen pious man of late, wearing orange among their garb. Is it a sign? A means to recognise your brethren? A badge of belonging?"

He tried to laugh, but his mouth was dry.

"Show me your wrists," she said.

He took a step back. "Why?"

Before he could react, she seized him and wrenched up his shirt sleeve.

There, on a leather thong, was tied an amber bead.

Their eyes locked. Eyes so alike in hue, they marked them as brother and sister.

William sank to his knees, clutching at her coat. "They're good men, Abby, with our Lord in their hearts. They took me in when I might have been executed. They…"

She held up a card before his face. A card bearing the number 3 beside a dancing flame.

"I received this," she said.

His face fell. "You… received it?"

She nodded. "You know what it means?"

His expression hovered between guilt and horror.

"The Righteous Flame are coming for me, William."

"Nay, Abigail, it can't be true. I told them… They promised me…"

Abby wrenched her coat from his grasp and stormed from the tent.

"Abigail!" he called after her. "I never meant… I swear to you, I'll make it right!"

But it was too late. She was gone.

Chapter Thirty-Nine

A Familiar Face

Unsteady on her feet, Abby cursed the tears that slid down her cheeks as she stumbled toward Barge House. She collided with folk - some calling after her, others shaking their fists - yet she neither slowed nor apologised.

Temple Street had offered shelter from the storm. Emerging at the southern end, she was struck by the full force of the blizzard. If anything, it had worsened.

The wind hurled the snow sideways, in sheets so thick she could see barely a few yards in front of her face. Tugging her collar tightly around her, she looked about for sign of Pepys and Jacob - but it was hopeless. They would never find each other in such a maelstrom.

Already, the plan was going awry.

A voice, bellowed into the elements, cut through the howling gale. It came from the direction of Barge House.

"The Lord in His mercy hath struck down the wicked, that ye may repent! Depart this sinful place, this den of vice, or grovel before His vengeance!"

Another Puritan, she thought, *aligned with the Righteous Flame.*

Yet there was something about this one.

Did she… *recognise his voice?*

She drew closer, his words rising over the storm.

"Is this icy tempest not God's wrath upon thee? Flee, you fools, lest ye be taken in His judgment!"

Gradually, a figure emerged through the whiteness: a figure clad in vermillion, features obscured by the mask of the Righteous Flame. This was the man she had seen with the placard, the one who had run away. She just knew.

When she stopped mere feet from him, he opened wide his arms, as if welcoming her in.

Time stopped. The gale, the clamour, seemed to quell.

Just her and him.

And she knew him.

Oh, how she knew him.

Even before he removed the mask.

She exhaled his name.

"Simon Hopkins."

He smiled. Long black hair and beard, and those dark, dark eyes and their malevolent stare.

"Abigail Harcourt." He sneered. "We meet again. I have been expecting you."

Of course he had. If Mortimer and Matthew Hopkins had been in cahoots, then why not Mortimer and Hopkins's son? The Puritan zealotry of the Righteous Flame came branded with the Hopkins name.

"Witch-finding lost its appeal?" she asked, and saw his expression harden. "I pleaded for your life, you know?"

It was true. After Hopkins had been caught using a false witch-pricking tool, attempting to frame Mr Pepys's sister as a witch, he might well have hanged. Yet Abby, with forgiveness in her heart, had petitioned Brampton's Senior Magistrate for leniency.

He smiled crookedly. "I required no pleas of a God-forsaken serving wench. The magistrate saw that I follow a righteous path."

"And now you follow the Righteous Flame."

The wind howled, and the snow scoured their faces.

"The Devil thrives when the righteous are shackled, Abigail. The Lord led me to His faithful - men who shall not suffer the godless to flourish."

"Your precious Righteous Flame have murdered men in their zealotry."

As she spoke, she noticed a man pass behind Hopkins, all but shrouded in snow. She felt certain it was Duke Hobbes.

Raising her voice, she added, "You plan to blast the ice asunder, Simon Hopkins! How many innocent lives will be lost?"

"'Tis but small price to pay, that the nation shall be saved."

She shook her head in disgust. "To think, I saved your life."

"And I owe you a debt." He paused, voice softening with mock sincerity. "However, today is not the day I repay it." Raising his hands, he clicked his fingers.

Instantly, two figures loomed through the blizzard and seized her, dragging her to the ice.

"…The Righteous Flame would ne'er permit its payment."

She managed to cry out, just once. "Jacob!"

But no reply came.

Chapter Forty

Barge House

Abby was carried up Barge House Stairs, the rotting timbers of the abandoned structure rising above her, groaning and clattering in the wind.

Her mind was awhirl and, like the snow, would not be stilled.

They followed the length of one wall, behind which barges were once stored, before veering toward a taller, adjacent building. Men passed by - garbed not in the robes of the Righteous Flame, but in threadbare coats and ragged cloaks - carrying wooden casks toward the river, faces drawn.

Hopkins kicked at a battered old door, sending it flying open.

Inside, the wind that had numbed her face fell away. The storm's roar dropped to a hush, and all fell eerily calm.

All, that is, save Abby's furiously beating heart.

These so-called righteous men, twisted, arrogant and fanatical, meant to murder her. She had the card that proved it.

And she knew it was no idle threat.

Chapter Forty-One

Temple Stairs

The brawl at the foot of Temple Stairs had attracted a crowd of onlookers. Some, drawn by the sport, or perhaps simply seeking warmth, threw themselves into the tussle.

Poor Mr Pepys, unaccustomed to such violence, moaned terribly as he was crushed beneath a heap of writhing bodies. His cheek was pressed into filthy slush, and his foot felt twisted behind him.

Then, suddenly, the weight lifted. Struggling to spy his saviour, he saw Jacob hoist the preacher to his feet and cast him aside as if he were a sack of coal.

However, when the inquisitor extended a hand to help him up, a pock-marked young fellow threw himself onto Jacob's back, pitching him forward. The pair landed on top of Pepys, who howled afresh

A tangle of elbows and knees jabbed at his body and head. The pain felt like it would never end.

Then, through the chaos, a sound emerged: a thin, rasping rattle.

A man's voice followed. "Ho there! Stop that at once, or I shall arrest you all!"

The constable, Archibald Frith, had arrived.

"Mr Frith! Mr Frith!" Pepys called out, his cries muffled by all those bodies, extracting a finger from his eye. "Help me!"

As Frith and his associates dragged men to their feet, Jacob saw his chance. Abandoning Pepys to his fate, he crawled quickly away from the mêlée, pushed himself upright and disappeared into the storm, around the side of the booths.

Briefly, guilt gnawed at him – should he return for his employer?

Nay, he decided. Abby's need was greater. Mr Pepys could deal with Archibald Frith.

The going was arduous, tracking the eastern edge of the tented street. He was in the teeth of the gale, battered by a wind that tore at his clothing and whipped over the booths, away toward Westminster.

Abby would have headed for Barge House, he knew, so that was where he was bound.

Chapter Forty-Two

The Flame

Barge House reeked of neglect and decay. Its ceiling rose high above Abby as she was manhandled inside, forced into a chair, and tied fast with rope.

Willing her nerves still, she took in her surroundings.

She was in a vast, empty timber hall, its walls darkened with damp and frosted with rime. Icicles as long as pikes and as thick as a man's arm hung from the rafters, among silent, nesting gulls. The windows were boarded up, and the only light came through cracks in the damaged structure, and from candles burning on iron stands placed around the floor.

In the centre of the room stood a brazier, its fire dancing, sparks skittering upwards.

A symbolic Righteous Flame? she wondered. *It looks rather... pathetic.*

Before the brazier stood three chairs, the central one tallest. Hopkins took the one on the right and stared at her mockingly.

Men were arriving, hoisting casks stacked against one wall onto their shoulders, and carrying them outside. She dared not wonder what their purpose might be.

Straining against her bonds, which would not give, she let out an anguished sigh.

An insistent, hollow tip-tapping drew her gaze toward the door.

A sullen-faced musician had entered, drumming on a tabor, leading a procession of masked and robed men. He sang a dirge-like psalm that echoed about the dilapidated space and sent a chill down Abby's spine.

Behind him came a tall, barrel of a man in a vivid orange robe, a thick chain of office around his neck. From it hung a medallion: a flame encircled by words she could not yet make out.

Mortimer, she assumed. Such trinkets would appeal to him.

Next came the only man dressed in white, the others – beside Mortimer – all wearing vermillion. In his hand, he carried a cane with a carved head in the shape of a flame.

When he saw her, he took head and cane in each hand and drew them apart. From its disguised sheath emerged a long, thin, vicious-looking blade.

It struck her at once: *the wound on Signor Napoli's neck.*

The white robe, the ghastly mask, the sword-stick – it all came together.

The Righteous Flame's executioner.

As the procession drew closer, Abby was able to read the words on Mortimer's medallion.

"He Shall Purge With Fire."

Hopkins stood as Mortimer took his seat, followed by the executioner, who settled to Mortimer's left.

More figures filed into the hall. Some short, some tall; most cast her a glance, bound to that chair. Others ignored her entirely, as if she failed to exist.

She met their looks with defiance, her heart thumping like a cartwheel over ruts.

One's gaze lingered longer than the rest. Distracted, he caught his foot on the hem of his robe and lurched into the man ahead.

"William?" she mouthed, but he turned his face away.

Two brethren approached and lifted Abby - chair and all - setting her down beside the flaming brazier. The others encircled it.

A church bell chimed its first of eight.

Mortimer rose, and they bowed their heads to pray.

Abby glanced toward the door for the umpteenth time. Still no Jacob.

"Abigail Harcourt, you have been chosen!" Mortimer intoned, rising and raising his arms to the heavens. "Your sacrifice will serve the Lord's will - I, High Warden of the

Righteous Flame, command it! And by your death, His warning shall be heeded!"

"His warning shall be heeded," the gathered voices echoed.

Abby strained against her bonds. "You should be in Bedlam!" she yelled. "All of you! Especially you, Tobias Mortimer!"

A few gasps rippled through the hall as every head turned to the man with the medallion.

Mortimer did not even acknowledge her taunt.

"This unholy fair casts a blight upon His name!" he droned. "The Righteous Flame shall purge these sinners from the ice!"

"The flame shall purge!" the brethren chanted.

"Cease this madness!" she cried, now frantic. "Murder a hundred men, and still more will come, laughing in the face of your cruel piety!"

With a flourish, Mortimer removed his mask, revealing an amused smirk. "Then perhaps we shall."

Abby rocked in her chair, hands curling into fists. "You'll never prevail."

She recoiled as he stepped forward, gripped the back of her chair and twisted it to face the stacked casks along the far wall.

"See there, girl. Gunpowder." The dread word reverberated around the empty building. "When the King comes - as surely he shall, lured by ego and vanity - we shall send him to the very pits of Hell, alongside all the other blasphemers who revel in this godless carnival."

"Nay!" she wailed.

Mortimer let out a single, mirthless laugh. "'Tis God's will, Abigail."

Replacing the mask, he raised his arms once again. "Let the execution commence!"

Chapter Forty-Three

The Guard

Jacob arrived at Barge House expecting a fight, yet found the area outside near deserted. Only one man lingered ahead – a solitary figure perched on a cask beside a door, striking a flint to his pipe.

The wind had eased some, though the snow still swirled in flurries. In his anguish, he barely felt the cold.

Where in God's name is Abby?

London's bells had some while ago tolled the eighth hour, and he was keenly aware he was late. Grimacing, he quickened his pace.

"Hold there!"

The man with the pipe had risen and was striding toward him. "State your business here," he demanded.

A guard.

When they were toe-to-toe, Jacob lifted his chin. "I seek a friend," he said.

"You'll find none here." The guard pushed him back. His nose was flat, and tufted hair sprouted from his rosy cheeks.

When Jacob stepped to one side, the guard mirrored him, blocking his path.

"I should leave?" Jacob asked.

The guard grunted. "Aye. On yer way, fellow."

Turning as if to go, Jacob swung back sharply, his fist connecting with the man's chin.

Down he went, cracking his head on the ice, and there he lay, motionless.

Jacob glanced around. No witnesses.

He hurried to the door the man had been guarding and pushed it open. The hinges groaned, but the sound was swallowed by a voice raging inside.

Jacob's gaze was instantly drawn to Abigail, and his heart leapt... until he saw she was bound to a chair, encircled by masked men in hooded robes. He fought the urge to cry out her name.

His next instinct was to charge in – but that would have been old-Jacob's way.

He was an inquisitor now.

And inquisitors made plans.

Chapter Forty-Four

A Wicked Plan

S ir Tobias Mortimer took great pleasure in detailing the ritual of Abby's execution.

Traditionally, he noted, the Righteous Flame's executioner - he gestured to his silent accomplice, the one in white with the sword-stick - would "perform the ceremony".

The thought struck her with disgust - such atrocities must have taken place before.

She longed to unleash her rage, but Mortimer had tired of her interruptions, and a gag now compelled her silence.

"On this occasion, however," he added, "I have a new executioner in mind. A man tied to your past. One whom you have aided with good heart."

To Mortimer's right, Hopkins stood.

Abby could not see his smile, hidden behind that blank leather mask, but she sensed it.

How dearly she wished she had let him swing.

Yet Mortimer bade Hopkins sit, and he dared not protest.

Instead, the High Warden of the Righteous Flame pointed to another among the circle.

On faltering steps, that man approached.

"Nay!" Abby tried to scream, but it emerged as a muffled, agonised cry.

A ceremonial dagger was produced – blackened steel, its blade rippled like flame – and placed in William Harcourt's trembling hand.

Facing Abby, he removed his mask.

In that moment, his blue-green eyes seemed to hold all the pain in the world.

She met his gaze, furiously shaking her head. "You don't have to do this!" she tried to urge him, but the gag warped her words into a desperate, garbled mess.

He raised the dagger high.

"Forgive me," he whispered. "But I serve God and Him alone." Then louder, for all to hear, he cried out, "The flame shall purge!"

Abby squeezed her eyes shut, bracing with every bone in her body, as he brought the weapon down in one sweeping arc…

Chapter Forty-Five

Demise

And sliced through her bonds.

"Run, Abby!" he urged.

Mortimer shot to his feet, flinging his mask aside with the roar of a wounded beast.

Hopkins, enraged, leapt from his chair and threw himself at William.

"Will!" Abby screamed, tearing off the gag.

He turned just in time.

The two men collided, William's dagger arm raised as Hopkins fought to wrench it from his grasp. They swayed one way then the other, locked in mortal combat - until William planted his feet, mustered his strength, and hurled his assailant onto his back.

Yet Hopkins clung on.

With a sickening crash, both men hit the floorboards, and, with a dreadful *crack*, the wood gave way.

In an instant, they were gone, plunged into darkness below.

Then: silence.

Abby rushed to the gaping hole and peered down.

Both men lay deathly still, limbs twisted at strange angles.

Hopkins's mask had slipped from his face, his vacant eyes staring up at her.

"Seize her!" Mortimer bellowed.

His executioner sprang into action, charging toward her, unsheathing his blade as he went.

All around her, the remaining brethren seemed trapped in mute consternation.

BOOOOM!

A blinding flash, followed by the stench of gunpowder.

Abby was hurled off her feet, mind reeling. Gasping for air, she lay sprawled on the floor. Her gaze drifted to the gaping hole in the far wall, then inexorably upward, to the rafters.

One of the huge icicles had cracked.

Mortimer must have sensed it too, since he looked up - just as it broke free.

He barely had time to scream.

Then was gone.

Chapter Forty-Six

Reckoning

The explosion had been a little louder than Jacob had anticipated. Having never worked with gunpowder before, he had been obliged to guess the quantity.

Still, as he burst through the hole he had blasted in the side of Barge House, the result was just as he had hoped.

Pandemonium and panic reigned. Hoods off, masks discarded, the brethren of the Righteous Flame shoved at each other's backs in a frantic bid to escape through the only door.

Sir Tobias Mortimer… he was done.

But where was Abby?

His gaze swept the wreckage, batting dust clouds aside.

Then he saw her.

Or rather, he saw the man in white first - arm raised, clutching a long silver blade, poised to plunge it into her quailing form.

"Ho!" Jacob bellowed, frantically waving his arms as he tore through the debris.

The executioner turned. One glance at the onrushing inquisitor, tall and manic, and he bolted for the door.

Jacob started toward Abby, but she frantically waved him on. "That's the man who killed Napoli," she yelled. "Don't let him escape!"

When Jacob burst outside, his quarry was fleeing toward Barge House Stairs, watched by several brethren only now rediscovering their senses.

"Ho!" he called again.

The executioner glanced back, lost his footing, and fell. Jacob pounded after him.

Out on the exposed river, he kept his sights on the fleeing figure, barely twenty yards ahead. His throat rasped with each icy breath.

Though the executioner's white cloak seemed to vanish into snow flurries at times, Jacob pressed on. This man, who had dared threaten his Abigail's life, would face justice.

Then, suddenly, his quarry stopped.

Instinctively, Jacob halted too.

As he did so, he became conscious, behind him, of the familiar, leaden beat of the drum boat.

Doomp . . . Doomp . . . Doomp . . .

How far across the river they had raced, he could not say, nor even where precisely they were. The storm seemed to swallow every landmark. Even Temple Street, to his right, built of so much beige canvas, was hard to make out.

Then he heard it, echoing from somewhere along the north bank: a trumpet fanfare.

He knew what it meant, and drew a sharp breath.

The King was coming.

As Jacob advanced, wary of his adversary's next move, he spotted the planks propped up on A-frames behind, and the darker ice beyond.

This was where the Dutchman had died.

"I know your game," he called out.

That unsettling mask and brandished sword might once have struck fear into him - but no longer.

The wind whistled as the King's fanfare sounded once more.

His Majesty was closer now. Perhaps even at Temple Stairs.

Rolling his shoulders, Jacob moved forward, each step a crisp crunch into crusted snow.

If only to calm his ripening nerves, he spoke again. "You murdered Signor Napoli. And tried to murder Mr Pepys."

Like Abby before him, he was piecing it together – and it stank like London's cesspits.

The man in white only stared.

"You may keep your mask and hood, sir, but by the design of that blade, you shall be recognised – and hanged."

That spurred the executioner. Blade-tip aimed at the inquisitor's heart, he lunged, but slipped on the slick surface. His feet flew from under him, his sword arm dropped, and Jacob felt a sharp pain at his ankle.

As Jacob toppled, he saw his adversary turn and sheath his weapon.

He hit the frozen Thames hard, the impact winding him.

The executioner drove the tip of his flame-topped sword-stick hard into the thin ice.

Jacob tried to get up, but his ankle gave way.

He could only watch, appalled, as the ancient river swallowed the weapon whole.

The executioner gazed across at him. Then, without a word, he ran.

Though Jacob tried to follow, a sharp, stabbing pain shot up his leg as he stood, and he sank back down.

When he looked again, his quarry had disappeared into the squall.

He slammed a fist into the frozen ground.

That was when he caught it. A sound – or rather, a silence – that jarred.

The drum boat's beat had ceased.

Chapter Forty-Seven

Final Voyage

Jacob lay on the frozen Thames, clutching at his ankle in agony and cursing his failure, as the royal fanfare grew ever closer.

He may have brought down the Righteous Flame, but the murderer had escaped, and his thoughts turned to Abby, whom he had abandoned in his haste.

What if Barge House collapsed?

Again he tried to rise, and again his ankle gave way as he cried out.

Then, he heard a strange grunting sound from behind.

Out of the hazy swirl emerged a figure, leaning forward at an acute angle, straining on a thick rope stretched over his shoulder and gripped in white knuckles.

"Hnnnn," went the man, inching forward, bellowing like a bull.

It was Duke Hobbes.

The rope angled upwards into the blizzard, disappearing into nothing - until the prow of the drum boat
appeared ghost-like through the white veil. Draped
over it was another man, arms dangling limply, a drum
still clinging to his neck.

Jacob recognised him, too. Horatio Carter.

"Ho! Ho! Mr Hobbes!" Jacob called out, waving.
"Hold, sir - the ice is open ahead!"

The fanfare sounded again. So close now that Jacob
peered out toward the north bank, half-expecting to
see the King himself appear.

To his relief, he did not.

When he turned back, Hobbes was crouching beside
him, holding out a well-laden leather purse.

"Take this," he said, and when Jacob failed to react,
snapped, "Hurry, man, take it! Make sure my men
get this money." He clamped Jacob's jaw in his big,
calloused hand, forcing their eyes to meet. "Tell me I
can trust you, sir. If not, believe me, my ghost shall
haunt you to your grave."

"A…Aye, sir," Jacob stammered. "But… What is
this?"

"The turncoat Carter's ill-gotten gains. They'll do
him no good now."

Jacob glanced again at the lifeless figure.

"You must move, sir, and quick," said Hobbes. "The
rogue lit a fuse in her hold and sealed the hatch - she's

set to blow." Then he noticed the seeping wound at the inquisitor's ankle.

Before Jacob could reply, Hobbes had dragged him to safety and was already loping back to his rope.

"What are you doing?" Jacob cried.

"This is my river, sir – and none shall besmirch it!"

As the ice cracked, the brave waterman went under in a fleeting moment.

The rope did not slacken. Even as he was taken by the fierce current beneath the surface, Hobbes knew to cling on.

The drum boat lurched onward, the ice groaned, the vessel pitched, tipped, then a great sheet of ice broke up beneath it.

Down it went, down into the dark water, releasing Carter into the depths and sinking itself, disappearing with a cacophony of *glugs* and *whooshes* into the river's chill embrace.

Jacob, saved from drowning by mere yards of solid ice, furiously propelled himself further from the bubbling chasm.

And there, standing at the brink of safety himself, he saw King Charles, flanked by uniformed men with pikes and muskets, staring at the broken river in abject horror.

Then, with a barked order, the King turned and was swallowed in the mists of snow.

Chapter Forty-Eight

New Year

January 1ˢᵗ, 1667

Mr Pepys was frankly appalled that Abby wished to invite Mr Evelyn and his companions back, to share their celebratory supper. But she was insistent and, since she and Jacob had foiled the Righteous Flame's diabolical plan, he was hardly able to refuse.

It had been two days since Pepys was rescued from the Frost Fair fracas by the constable, Archibald Frith, and his men. At Pepys's urging, his rescuers had seen fit to investigate the sinister goings-on at Barge House, and were halfway across the river when Jacob's explosion lit up the sky. That they had travelled downriver of Temple Street meant they had missed the drum boat's demise in its aftermath.

Jacob, returning for his fellow inquisitor on a crutch fashioned from debris, had been denied entry by Frith, whose volunteers had found Abby wandering outside the collapsing ruin. So shaken were its foundations by the blast that it was pulled down the following day.

Jacob escorted Abby all the way back to Pepys's house, teeth gritted against the pain in his leg, where she had been allowed to recover.

She never spoke of her brother.

The Yule log, which had taken two men to carry up the stairs, still glowed in the fireplace and would last until Twelfth Night. The evergreen adornments remained in place, still offering their heady scent of Christmastide, even as one year slid into another.

The table groaned under the weight of the food – such a display as might be captured for posterity in a painting.

A goose, roasted and stuffed, formed the centrepiece. Around it were arranged dishes of boiled mutton with oysters, cold beef, venison pie, baked leeks and onions, buttered carrots and parsnips, winter salad… a feast for all the senses.

"Are you enjoying the Frost Fair, Sam?" John Evelyn asked, breaking one of several lingering silences.

Pepys glanced up from his plate, eyeing Jacob, then Abby, and finally Evelyn. "Aye, John," he replied. "How marvellous it has been for London to emerge from those dark days of plague and fire." His tone was flat.

After a significant pause, broken only by the sound of chewing, he added, "And you, John?"

Evelyn set down his knife. "My garden at Sayers Court is all but dead," he said.

Jacob nudged Abby and raised his eyes skyward.

Arthur Baines caught him doing so, and smirked. "Where is your wife, Mr Pepys?" he asked. "She did not grace us with her presence at Christmastide and is once again noticeable by her absence. I trust we," he gestured toward Barker and Evelyn," have not offended her somehow?"

Pepys's irritated growl was masked by the chimes of St Olave's bell, notifying the seventh hour. He had opened his mouth to reply when a commotion of falling pots and pans erupted from the kitchen below, followed by Mary Blythe's cursing.

Scowling, Pepys rose, then sat back down as footsteps sounded on the stairs.

Mary appeared at the top, breathless.

"I do beg your pardon, sir," she said. "The cat found its way in again and toppled my shelves. Do pray forgive me. I've slung it out."

"Hmm," Pepys muttered. "Very well. Now begone, will you."

As she departed, the maid shot Abby a wink.

"What of your family, Mr Baines?" Abby piped up. "How many children was it that you have?"

Baines narrowed his eyes and forced a laugh. "As I told you before, I have so many delightful offspring, 'tis a burden to remember them all." He looked to Evelyn for affirmation, who managed a half-smile.

Jacob and Pepys reached for their goblets at the same time, noticed it, and both drew back.

Barnaby Barker, oblivious to the general tension, tore off a goose leg.

Spearing a carrot, Abby returned her attention to Baines. "You asked after my family on Christmas Day. Why was that?"

"Out of politeness," he replied, bemused. "It seems my effort was wasted."

Pepys glared at Abby, but it did not stop her. "You reside in Deptford?" she asked Baines. When he nodded, she continued, "And you have five… I beg your pardon, six sons?"

Baines chuckled mirthlessly, his expression darkening. "What is the meaning of this interrogation?"

"You seemed keen to interrogate Mr Pepys concerning the King's position on the Dutch War, did you not?"

"A plague upon your insolence, girl!" Baines thumped the table. "Know your place!"

"Enough, Abigail," Pepys chimed in. "Mr Baines is my guest and does not wish to be questioned by you."

Before she could apologise, Baines rose abruptly and strode toward the privy. Just as he reached the doorway, Abby called out, "Mr Wrathbone?"

For the briefest of instants, Baines faltered.

"What is your game, Abigail?" Pepys demanded, while Evelyn looked on in discomfort and Barker swallowed an oyster. "'Tis most unseemly. I…"

"Do you trust me, sir?" she asked.

Pepys shrugged. "Why, indeed. You are a most proficient inquisitor."

"Then I beg your indulgence a while longer."

The silence in the room ached as Baines retook his seat. Only Mr Barker was eating.

Baines had barely settled when Abby spoke again.

"When last you dined here, Mr Baines," she said, "you wore a cravat the colour of flame. Yet not this night. Is it… lost?"

He could only glare.

Jacob was finding it hard to contain himself. The inquisitors had planned for this moment, and he was finding it more delicious than the goose.

"When we met at The Duke of York's Coffee House on Temple Street," Abby continued, "you seemed keen that Mr Evelyn not accompany us to the printer's booth…"

Baines spluttered. "I recall it not! This is preposterous!" An eyelid flickered. "And what of it if I did?"

"Perhaps Mr Evelyn already knew the printer, having met him in Deptford? Which Jacob and I would then discover?"

"Abigail, what…?" Pepys began.

But Evelyn spoke over him, clasping at Baines's arm. "Arthur, why does she ask these questions? Indeed I do know the printer – he is your son, William."

Chapter Forty-Nine

Triumph

"His *adopted* son, Mr Evelyn," Abby corrected him. "Also my brother, William Harcourt."

Evelyn sat bolt upright, blinking in confusion. "I understood the lad had been adopted, Arthur told me so. But I was led to believe his family name was Wrathbone."

"Nay, sir. Will's family name is Harcourt. He's my brother."

She went on to recall that Baines had arrived for dinner on Christmas Day clutching a leather satchel. "I assumed its initials - 'H.W.' - were the maker's mark. They weren't, were they, Hezekiah Wrathbone?"

Baines shot to his feet, fingers digging into the table's edge, as if about to heave it over. Then he caught himself, inhaled deeply, and growled, "Mr Pepys, how long will you suffer this impertinent stream of conjecture and falsehood? It taints my good name and casts aspersions upon your own." Baring his teeth at Abby, he demanded, "Where is your proof, girl?"

All eyes turned to her.

"You hide your Puritan fervour well, Mr Wrathbone." Abby paused. "You have a cane, I believe? We saw you with it, at Temple Stairs on the first day of the Frost Fair. You shielded its head from us in your gloved hands." She turned to her fellow inquisitor. "Jacob?"

Reaching under the table, he produced a sturdy cane, topped with a flame-shaped carved head.

Baines, face darkened to a violent shade of puce, could only croak, "How?"

Jacob recounted asking the constable where the Dutchman's body had been found, when it was carried by the current from the very same place Napoli's murderer had ditched his sword-stick.

"Where was that, Jacob?" Abby asked, eyes twinkling.

"Down by the Fleet at Bridewell, where the rivers meet. I walked there yesterday and found it tangled in weeds."

"What in Heaven's name is it, Abigail?" Pepys asked.

"It belongs to the Righteous Flame's executioner, sir, it…"

Baines hurled his empty goblet across the room. "And ne'er have I set eyes upon it!"

Abby sighed. "But you have, Mr Wrathbone, and Jacob and I would testify to it. But that won't be necessary.

You're a fastidious man, are you not? Your satchel bears your initials, as did the chisel Jacob found beside poor Signor Napoli... once we had turned it over."

She shot a glance at her fellow inquisitor, who had assured them the chisel's initials were M.H. He avoided her gaze – indeed, they would have read 'H.W.' if inverted.

"Then it struck me..." Abby continued, taking the cane and holding its head under Pepys's nose. "Sir, do you see initials engraved there, below the flame's tip."

Pepys clasped it, peering. "I do. H... W. What is the meaning...?"

Abby explained that the Righteous Flame had colluded with Dutch spies, to rid England of its King - a mutually beneficial arrangement. It was the Dutchmen who had employed Horatio Carter to pack the drum-boat with gunpowder, timed to detonate on King Charles's arrival.

"Mr Wrathbone here would return us to the days of Cromwell," she concluded. "He and his Puritan kinfolk do so hate seeing the people enjoy themselves."

In one swift movement, Baines leapt onto the table, scattering jugs and dishes, and seized the cane from a stunned Abby.

As he unsheathed the long blade, Mr Barker rose, gripped Baines's ankles in both hands, and hauled him back.

Down Baines went, his head smacking into the heavy oak tabletop, as the sword flew from his grasp and skittered across the floor, coming to rest by the fire.

And there he lay, unconscious, one hand draped in the syllabub dish.

"I cannot bear Puritans," said Barker, and sat down.

They were his first words that Christmastide.

The heavy thumping of booted feet approached up the stairs and a wide-eyed Archibald Frith appeared, wheezing, followed by a pair of accomplices. "It appears I am too late," he noted drily.

Pepys tore off his periwig, shaking his head. "Abigail Harcourt, would you please explain what is happening here!"

She had, she said, invited the constable to join them at the seventh hour, ready to arrest Baines. Mary's tumbling pots and pans had masked the sound of his entry. "There was no cat, sir," she added.

Though she was supposed to give a signal, Baines had been too quick for her. Instead, Mr Barker had come to the rescue.

While a groggy Baines was hauled from the table by Frith's men, Evelyn interjected. "I confess I am most perplexed, Mistress Harcourt. Is that man Arthur Baines or Hezekiah Wrathbone? I was aware I knew him not well, but it appears I knew him not at all."

"I believe he changed his name to Baines when he moved to Deptford," Abby replied, "Probably evading justice from his nefarious activities."

"And why did you suspect him?" Pepys pressed.

"You remember saying it was just I to whom you'd mentioned the King's loathing of cold weather? Thus the unlikelihood of His Majesty attending the puppeteer's Command Performance?" When Pepys nodded, she continued, "But it wasn't just me you told. You announced it to the table, at our first dinner with Mr Evelyn and his associates. Baines also knew - and 'tis why the Italian had to die."

Chapter Fifty

One was Dead

While Arthur Baines - Hezekiah Wrathbone - was being shackled, Abby found the opportunity to take Mr Barker to one side.

"You heard everything," she hissed in his ear. "Yet we were told you're deaf."

Barker winked and nodded toward Evelyn. "I feign it to quell his discourse. My grandson can be such a bore," he whispered. "If ne'er I hear about another orchid…"

A chair scraped across the floor as Pepys rose.

Baines was being dragged to the stairs when Pepys called to Frith, "Hold, pray." He turned to Baines. "I would know, sir - why would you have me blamed for the Dutchman's murder?"

Baines's lip curled in contempt. "Since it amused me, Samuel Pepys, knowing you had suffered a similar fate at the King's court only days before. And since you are among the basest of men, a lecher, a libertine, and a user of whores." His voice rose and his eyes burned with righteous fury. "God's wrath shall come for you, sir, and on that judgment day you shall…"

"Aye, you may take him away now, Mr Frith!" Pepys called over him.

The constable watched as his men departed, then rapped his fist against the wall. "'Tis time," he called downstairs. "You may join us now."

Jacob and Abby exchanged puzzled glances as footsteps ascended the stairs.

"I discovered two men in the basement of Barge House," Frith said. "One was dead. The other has made a most remarkable recovery."

"Will?" Abby gasped, hands flying to her cheeks.

"I wasn't sure you'd wish to see me," said Will Harcourt, stepping into view.

"Will! Oh, Will!" Abby cried, flinging herself at him. "You're alive!"

Pepys and Jacob looked on, beaming proudly.

Jacob leaned toward Pepys and murmured, "I trust Abby's newfound happiness shall not preclude us from our inquisitors' duties, sir."

"I hope so also, Jacob," Pepys replied. "Have you ever had occasion to visit the King's Playhouse in Drury Lane?" When Jacob indicated otherwise, Pepys patted his arm. "You shall do so, soon enough…"

If you enjoyed this book, please consider leaving a rating or review – they are greatly appreciated and genuinely help.

Next up: Abby goes undercover as principal actor at the King's Playhouse, in The Samuel Pepys Mysteries Book 6: The Drury Lane Murders.
Amazon link: mybook.to/pepys-series

- "This series just gets better with every book" – *Rambling Mads*

- "A brilliant mix of history and fiction - I loved every minute" – *What You Tolkein About*

- "Abby is my absolute favourite – her portrayal as a headstrong woman in this period makes me smile." – *My Book Journey*

READ ALL NINE!

mybook.to/pepys-series

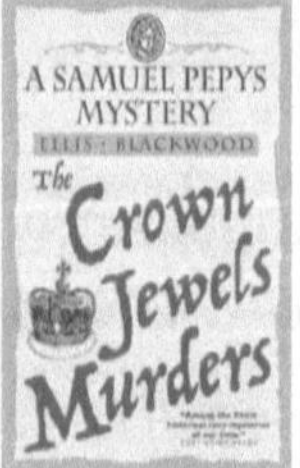

Ellis Blackwood

Ellis Blackwood fell in love with the writings of Samuel Pepys and the 17th-century England he so colourfully portrays via the great man's published diaries. The Samuel Pepys Mysteries are the result of that literary love affair.

Ellis lives on the coast of Cornwall with his wife, two daughters and dog, Spike. A former journalist, he wrote features for many of the UK's most popular national newspapers and magazines. During the COVID lockdown, he gained an MA in Comedy Writing.

Visit my website ellisblackwood.com for all release updates, and to subscribe to my monthly newsletter – including the FREE Pepys Mysteries introductory novella, Mr Pepys's Stolen Diaries.

Find me on Facebook @ellisblackwoodauthor
And on Instagram @ellisblackwood_author
Scan the QR code for all my links.

Acknowledgements

I could not have published The Samuel Pepys Mysteries without the sterling work of Tim Brown, whose covers are a joy to behold, and whose editorial guidance has been a godsend. Equally, my wife, Sinead, has worked tirelessly and generously in the background to allow me the time and space to research, write, and drink far too much tea.

If you'd like to learn more about Samuel Pepys and 17th century England, I recommend starting here:

- *The Illustrated Pepys* edited by Robert Latham, Penguin Books (1979)

- *London and the 17th Century* by Margarette Lincoln, Yale University Press (2021)

- *Samuel Pepys: The Unequalled Self* by Claire

Tomalin, Penguin Books (2003)

- *The Time Traveller's Guide to Restoration Britain* by Ian Mortimer, The Bodley Head (2017)

In my monthly newsletters, I deep-dive into the fascinating historical background to each novel, from the Princes in the Tower to the ingredients of posset. Visit ellisblackwood.comto sign up.

www.ingramcontent.com/pod-product-compliance
Lightning Source LLC
Chambersburg PA
CBHW031255120726
47906CB00003B/756